HEAR THE SILENCE

HEAR THE SILENCE

Stories by Women of Myth, Magic & Renewal

EDITED BY IRENE ZAHAVA

THE CROSSING PRESS
Trumansburg, New York 14886

Grateful acknowledgement is made for permission to use the following previously published material:

"Why The Sea Is Salty," by Kitty Tsui. Originally appeared in *Common Lives/Lesbian Lives*. Copyright © 1982 by Kitty Tsui, reprinted by permission.

"Fruit Drink," by Bode Noonan. Originally appeared in *Red Beans and Rice: Recipes for Lesbian Health and Wisdom*, by Bode Noonan, The Crossing Press. Copyright © 1986 by Bode Noonan, reprinted by permission.

"Sticktalk," by Vickie L. Sears. Originally appeared, in somewhat different form, in *Gathering Ground: New Writing and Art by Northwest Women of Color*, edited by Jo Cochran, J.T. Stewart and Mayumi Tsutakawa, The Seal Press. Copyright © 1984 by Vickie L. Sears, reprinted by permission.

"She Unnames Them," by Ursula K. Le Guin. Originally appeared in *The New Yorker Magazine*. Copyright © 1985 by *The New Yorker Magazine*. Reprinted by permission of the author and the author's agent, Virginia Kidd.

For my teachers:
Yetta, Eve, Laura, Martha, Meg, Babs, Linda

Contents

Preface

In the last five years my work in a feminist bookstore has brought me into contact with a widely divergent group of women. Some belong to covens and celebrate pagan holidays by performing group rituals. Others burn incense and light candles; some practice yoga, meditate or study T'ai Chi Ch'uan. Some chant. Many have created personal altars in their homes. Quite a few study goddess lore and matriarchal cultures. A few pray. A few others are atheists. There are members of church congregations and those who attend Synagogue. There are a number of ex-Catholics, non-religious Protestants and non-observant Jews. Some do absolutely nothing that they define as spiritual; others identify as being part of a women's spirituality movement. A couple laugh at the very mention of those words.

It was my aim, in working on this book, to gather a collection of short stories — of *spiritual* stories — that would appeal to all these women. I wanted this book to convey a sense of the innumerable ways spiritual awareness operates in our lives — even if those aren't the words we use to describe our own experiences.

The characters in these stories are bus drivers, cooks, basket-weavers, social workers, children, and beings from another planet — in settings as diverse as Philadelphia, Northwestern Canada, New Orleans, the California desert and the Swiss Alps. Some of these stories can easily be identified with the broadest definition of spirituality. Others are so subtle that you have to look between the words to see that slight shimmer of cosmic consciousness. All of them, I feel, have the potential to reveal another truth; one which lies just beyond the surface of our daily lives. It is what you learn when you listen for — and hear — the silence.

Irene Zahava
June, 1986

Magic in a World of Magic

ANNE CAMERON

First

*I*t is the custom of the People that when a story has been told to you, you give the teller something of equal value; a story of your own. And so it often is, the storytellers meet and first one will tell a wonderful tale, and another will share with a second wonderful tale. The first will be so moved by the story of the second that she will offer a third wonderful tale, and on hearing the third tale, the second teller will be so moved she will offer a fourth tale. Then a passer-by, hearing one of the stories, will seat herself with the storytellers, and she will share. And soon, there they are, sitting in the central compound, telling stories, one after the other, forgetting everything except the stories and the joy of telling, and though their throats parch and their voices become hoarse, all are loathe to leave the storytelling circle, and they might starve, or perish of thirst if it were not for the mercy of the People, who bring them water, and food, and if it is cold, light the poor fools a fire while they spin their yarns and keep alive the songs, the riddles, the tales, the stories, those things which are our only touch to that other place, where we will all go one day, but not for a long time, I fear.

It is the custom of the People that when a story has been told it belongs to the one who told it, not the one or ones who heard it. Nobody would tell a story not given to her, the sin of it is too great, the shame of it too enormous. And so it is, a storyteller tells a story and if she does *not* say "and now you can tell that story," you must never repeat it, but hold it in your heart, and cherish it, consider it, think about it, learn from it. For a story is like a flower, a precious fragility in itself, and you may take apart that flower and examine it, and you perhaps might press it between the pages of a book if you have one, or you may store it, dried, in a potpourri jar, but what you have is no longer the flower, it has become something else altogether, and so it is with a story. Told without permission, the story loses its magic benefit and becomes only a lie, and a stolen lie at that. And so I ask you, with these stories, hold them in your heart as you would the memory of a flower, but do not take them for your own, nor repeat them, nor presume to teach them or demonstrate by your appropriation how great the gap is between us, for if you take what is not given, you demonstrate only how ignorant you are of what it is you have heard, you demonstrate only how much you have not learned, you demonstrate how far you have to travel to be worthy of having the stories given you, you insult yourself.

These are some of the stories of the one who is known as The Changed, and sometimes known as The Changer, and sometimes known by no name at all, and I tell you these stories but I do not give them to you for they are the stories of my people, my people who are The People, and if I give them to you, what then will we have, we who are, as is well known, the poorest of creatures on the face of this world, we who own nothing and aspire to nothing, we who once had it and now have lost it and deem it well lost, we who once walked the surface of this world free and now cannot move without our Permit and our Pass and our Dispensation and our Identity Bracelets.

A word I will use often in telling these stories is "Unremarkable." Please do not think I use it only because my vocabulary is restricted, or because they did not take the time at residential school to teach me properly, because they were good to us in that place, and fed us at least as well as they fed their animals, often even the same food, and they were as kind to us as they knew how to be and only beat us senseless when it was for the good of our souls. I use the word "Unremarkable" because that is what the People say of The Changed, that in most of the things of her life, she was as ordinary as any of us, as unremarkable as any of us, with nothing extraordinary about her at all except, of course, the effect she had on others.

My mother sent me here, to this storytelling circle, with this fruit for you, and this loaf of fresh-baked bread, and she told me to give this to you, and to give you, also, this jug of juice, for indeed she said, your throats must be dry after a full day exchanging wisdom. My mother said I was to tell you your stories have helped fill the holes in the fabric of her own inheritance, for she had never before understood some of the things you have explained with your tales. My mother says she recognizes the cloth tied to your left arm, and recognizes you are members of the guild of storytellers, and she knows it is an honor to be accepted as an apprentice, and that if you decide at any time to offer apprenticeship to any of her children, my mother will be proud, prouder than if her children were to become merchants or traders or even officials of the sub-government. Praise, she says, to your guild, to you, and to the work you do. And she says I should explain to you why it is she sends me, her only daughter, to sit beside you in the square and give you stories which are not mine, but my mother's. She has sent me to be her throat, and her voice, and her tongue, for she herself has none.

My mother was one of the People who live outside the walls of the towns, and was taken, as a child, and put into Protection, and sent to a school, and at that time she tried to swallow her tongue, or stop her breathing, or send her spirit from her body, or any of the things the Untamed do when captured, but she always found herself back in her body, and finally, because she was only a child and possibly did not understand the teachings, she thought perhaps it was not intended that she be free, perhaps it was not intended that she pass over yet, and so she stopped trying.

In the school they would not let her talk the language of the People, but taught her the language of the Authorities, and instead of learning to guard the herds or work with her hands in the plots of earth, she was taught to work in the kitchen, taught to sew clothes for other people, and taught to understand the printouts that demanded when it was time for the machines to work the earth, plant the seeds, spread the chemical, and spray the insect and weed poison.

When she was fourteen, as happens to almost every woman of the People except those who are either cursed or blessed, one of the Authority men looked at her and she was taught all about that, too, and wondered for a long time what it was about her, or in her, or in the way she behaved, or in the things she did or did not do that attracted him and urged him to do the many things he did, none of which she enjoyed, most of which she found frightening, shameful, unpleasant and guilt-inducing, some of which hurt her body as well as her spirit, some of which were so painful she wept.

When she was almost twenty, and that first man had been replaced by another man who had made the choice without giving her any choice, she found herself to be pregnant. And the man was angry, for he had ordered her to take the injections and she had done it but he did not believe her and so he beat her, and in the beating, he swung his arm and hit her across the throat. Blood began to pour from her mouth, enough blood that he was frightened and took her to the Infirmary. And there are People who say my mother ought to have Passed Over then, for she was badly hurt and we are frail vessels intended to pass over at the slightest crack, but my mother had no more success passing over then than she had when she was a child taken into protective care.

They stopped the blood, and she recovered, but her voice was gone, and so her stories were locked inside her and she could give nothing back to the storytellers except food and drink and sometimes a bed and a place to stay.

That child was lost, for when they worked to stop the

bleeding inside her throat, they also vacuum extracted the child, and my mother did not even know until weeks later.

When she got out of hospital she went to work on one of the farms, and she tended the great herds, and met one of the men of the People. He was a man who did not find my mother unnatural because she had not passed over when damaged, and with him, when they had some monies saved, she moved to this walled town, and he made his living with weaving, and she is known in this town and several others, as a fine silversmith, maker of bracelets and rings, and even in the City her work is sought after and desired.

They had sons, and I am the only daughter, and my mother has taught me signs with the hands, and so it is we can communicate, and she has given me many stories, but there is much she cannot tell me for she is only herself inventing the talking fingers and there is so much we have not yet learned to exchange.

Sometimes my mother writes her stories on paper for me to read, but much is lost that way, especially when you cannot see the expression on the face of the storyteller, or see the language of the body movements.

Of course, when my mother was young, and taken into protective custody, she had not had time enough with the People to hear or remember many of the stories, and once she was in the school, surrounded by other liberated children and under the supervision of the Authorities, the telling of stories was prohibited. Even talking the language of the Untamed was prohibited, and the punishments were severe. My mother, having been raised wild, knew nothing of the language of the Civilized Authorities, and at first, confused and frightened, appealed to the older children to explain things to her. And, of course, she appealed to them in her own language. Each time she was heard or overheard, and each time the punishment was more severe, because, of course, each time they checked their records, and each time saw that here was a child who had already been punished once, twice, three, four, five, a dozen times. Finally, my mother learned enough of the Civilized language she no longer had to use her own, and with the need gone, the punishments stopped, and the Authorities were pleased to have taught her respect for them and their rules.

In spite of all the education, in spite of the vigilance of the Authorities, a few old stories circulated, and, as ignorant as children always are, the stories were more attractive than the learning tapes. Even translated into the Civilized language, even bled of the words that describe sixteen kinds of wind and thirty-two kinds of sunny day, even without the words to describe scents and colors, even without the proper knowledge of the influence of dreams, or the symbolism of visions, the stories caught at the minds of the children, and they repeated them to each other, sometimes editing from them, sometimes adding to them, until the stories, though still the same stories, were changed and altered and became new stories, and the new stories were told and re-told and edited and gave birth to other stories.

Every year new children were brought into care, and they brought with them other stories, or fragments of stories, and these, too, were told in the language of the Authorities, and re-told and added to and edited from and sometimes invented.

Because they were children, and unable to understand, they did some foolish things. Now we all know "Diddycoy" is a dirty word, that it comes from the word Indigenous, and that no person with integrity would use the word or answer when it was used to call her, and we all know "Diddycoy" gets shortened to "Coy," which is not so evil a word but still means the same as the other. And we all know it is an insult. But in their stories, the stupid children, possibly because of innocence, possibly because of ignorance, used both words freely. Until the words became new words with different meanings, and now, when those children are called by those names, instead of being insulted, or hurt, or shamed, or diminished, they remember the storytelling times and how they had found a way to keep alive what the Authorities had almost killed, and done that which was forbidden, and saved that which otherwise might have been lost, and they even feel a thing they call pride. Which they

6

say is a warm feeling much like love, and which, they tell me, makes you feel as if what you would really like to do is laugh, even if there is no reason.

My mother tells me she has felt this feeling. And she says she felt it when living in a small village with my father. There was a woman arrived at the village, and nobody knew it at the time, but the woman, who called herself Meg, was, in fact The Changer. An unremarkable woman, a woman like any other, a woman like myself, or like yourself, or like any woman you have ever seen.

She was of a certain age, then; not old, perhaps, but no longer young, and there were lines at the corners of her eyes, and lines cut into her face where her smile fit, and like many of us, her hands were large, and one look at them and you knew she was used to work, oh yes indeed, used to hard work, manual labor, and her knuckles were swollen, her fingers thick, and along the edge of both hands, from where her wrist ended to the very tip of her little finger, all along that outer edge, a thick callous, and she thrilled the children by breaking planks with one blow, and demonstrating to them how to practice until they could crumble a brick, how even to break small trees, and when it was time for an animal to be turned into food, it was this Meg who would move toward it, talking softly, calming it, thanking it, singing praises to it, and then, before the animal had a hint of what was about to happen, the hand would flash, and the edge of that calloused palm would connect and what had been an animal was food, and no blood spilled to frighten the other animals.

With those same hands she could soothe a frightened child, or play her instrument, which she called a lute, and she laughed with us often, and would play with the children kicking a ball back and forth or guarding the goal and keeping the ball from going in, whatever the game, it was Meg would play like a large laughing child, and jokes, oh my yes, jokes, she listened to them and laughed and told them and laughed and sometimes, she even lived them.

There was a man living in the village who lusted after the

children. Not to eat, oh my no, not to eat, but to warm his bed and please his passion. And it does not matter if this man was of the People or of the Authorities or if he was Mixed or if he was Outcast, or whatever, no indeed, it does not matter at all, for some in every group are like that man, and the hunger has nothing to do with anything we would understand or want to understand, and Meg asked why we allowed this, and we told her we had no idea what to do, for, as we all know, as the Authorities explained when they civilized us, a child does not always tell everything that happens, and anyway, nobody had *seen* this man do any of these things, and nobody knew for certain, and in any event, was there anything could be done, and if there was, it was nothing anybody could see, for talking to the man did no good and nobody has ever been sure what to do with a crazy, and anyway perhaps the man himself was merely doing to others what had been done to him, and if so, who could judge him, and besides, it was just too awful to think about, far better to spend time and energy considering nice things, and so the man continued to do what he had done for years.

Now one day this man went out of his house and there was Meg sitting by his woodpile, waiting and watching and smiling and the man said And what is it you want? Well, she said, I have come to learn something. Oh, he said, and have you indeed? And what is it you want to learn, would it be chopping wood? No, she said, I know how to chop wood, and I know how to draw water, and I even know how to find water if it is scarce, and I know enough to feed myself and keep myself alive, what it is I have come here to learn is why it is you play with the bodies of children. Well, said the man, go away, don't talk to me like that, who are you that you would dare ask such a question?

Who am I, she said, who am I. Well, she said, I will tell you. My name is Meg, as if that matters, and I am the one who is asking you why it is you lust after children.

You mean, said the man, you mean you really want to know? Oh, yes, said Meg, because surely in all my life and all my travels I have never had any suggestion of a reason I could understand, and I am becoming an old woman and would not want, she said, to die in such infernal ignorance.

Well, said the man, if you must know, it is their soft skin. Oh, said Meg, soft skin is it. Well, then, by all means, the more of it you have, the happier you will be. And she began to call very loudly Bring this man some young rabbits, bring him the softest you can find.

You fool, the man laughed, you stupid fool, it is not just their soft skin, it is their innocence, too. Innocence said Meg, oh, would that be like vulnerability, and the man said Yes, yes, it would, and Meg said Oh. And she said Would that be like helplessness, and the man said well, not exactly, but almost, and Meg said It sounds as if what you are saying is you do not want some capable woman, or some independent woman, and the man said No, he said No I certainly do not want any such thing, and Meg said Well, I have heard of that before, but never to such a degree as what you show, although I must admit it seems to me as if a sheep would do just as well, and she began to yell Hold the rabbits, bring this man a sheep.

Stop it, the man said, you are too stupid for words, it is not sheep I want, it is children. Well, said Meg, I have misunderstood again, forgive me, I am trying to understand. So it is more than soft skin and helplessness and mindlessness that you need. Yes, said the man, it is trust, too. Oh, trust, said Meg, trust indeed, and she began to shout in a voice that was so loud it was heard throughout the village Bring this man everything that is trusting, for he is mad with passion for such things, bring him kittens and puppies, bring him baby chicks and

Stop it, said the man, for God's sake stop it, you are too stupid to be endured, you are ruining my life, you are driving me crazy. Besides, he said, look at all these people who have come here bringing sheep and puppies and goats and all of them laughing. You are an evil woman, he said, an evil wicked woman and you are stupid and ugly as well.

I am only trying to understand, Meg explained, and she told him if more people could understand, perhaps they would not whisper about him behind his back or tell their children to stay away from him. Well, said the man, there is their soft skin, and their innocence, and their trust, and there is also their passivity. Oh, said Meg, passivity! Now that, she said, I can understand. I have met many passive things. And she began to yell Bring this man pieces of wood and pieces of dung, and bits of grass, and old cloth, bring this man dead meat and bring this man potatoes and rice, and she called for all manner of passive things, and the people brought them, and gave it to the man, standing back somewhat and tossing the offerings to him, and he stood with turnip peelings hanging from his ears and bits of old fruit spattered on his clothes, and rocks lumping his head, and sticks flying everywhere.

Stop it, he said, you are trashing me, Oh, said Meg, I do not intend that, I am trying to learn. Learn, the man screeched, look what you have done, the entire world throws things at me and knows about my lust for children and you, you ugly old fart, you stand there laughing, and she said but I am not laughing at you, I am laughing at *them!*

What is there to laugh at, the man moaned, look what you have done to me, all my secrets exposed to public view, and no child will come near me again, and if I move to another village, still the story of what you have done here will get around and I might as well be dead.

Oh, it's not that bad, Meg soothed, and the man screamed Not that bad, it's worse, and you don't even understand my suffering. Oh, said Meg, suffering is it, well I understand that, for in my own childhood, you see, I encountered a man such as yourself and everything you did to these children in this village he did to me, and it all hurt very much, and I wept, and I fought, and none of that did any good so finally I did nothing at all, not even tell anyone else about it, and I certainly never did understand any of it, which is why I have come to study with you, for surely the suffering I experienced has to have an explanation.

Go away, he moaned, and she said Oh, I cannot do that or I will never understand, I will just stay here and chop wood for

10

you and make meals for you and see to it these people bring things to you, and see to it you have as much of what it is you say you want that you won't have to chase children into bushes but can spend all the hours of your days and nights explaining to me why it was my blood and my pain was erotic.

Oh God, he screeched, I wish I were dead. What's that you say, Meg asked, what is it you say you want? I wish I were dead, he screamed, oh, I wish I never again had to endure any of this. Oh well, said Meg, if you are sure that is your most heartfelt desire, and he wept and assured her it was.

Now Meg never did come to an understanding of that man's strange desires, but she did manage, with the callous alongside the palm of her hand, to give him what it was he said he wanted. And in that village, at least, the children are safe.

And my mother, whose throat was damaged and whose voice was stilled, saw this happen, and has given me this story to share with you, for she, too was taken as a child and never understood any of the reasons, and she, too, has long searched for a reason, and found none, and when she saw Meg's gift to the man, when she saw the flash of movement that gave the man what he said he wanted, my mother said she suddenly understood so many things, and she smiled widely, and knew that were any man to ever make a move toward her daughter, my mother, too, would give what Meg had given.

Second

Any of you have only to look at me and you will know I am not of your people, who call themselves The People. Any one of you have only to look at me and you will know that my people came here from elsewhere and are people you call Authorities.

My mother, years ago, when I was barely old enough to have memories, left my father, for reasons she has never explained, and, having left him, left also the city, that one city of which we know, that one city which may well be the only city although it is said that in that Other Place, there were so many cities they merged, and several cities became one large city and reached out toward even other cities.

With the city well behind her, my mother travelled for many years, and then, for reasons she has never explained, chose this village as the place where she would live. She had some money, and with it she opened an inn, and on the third and second floors were rooms she rented to travellers or to those who prefer not to have to look after a house of their own. We lived on the bottom floor, but our quarters were well and safely separated from the large room where food and drink was served, and I slept near the kitchen, where the food was stored and prepared. She hired one of the People to prepare food for those passers-by who preferred the cooking of your people, and on those rare times when someone asked for the food of the Authorities, my mother prepared the meal, and those people have always said my mother is an excellent cook. I, myself, grew to prefer the spices and hot sauces of the People, and my mother saw nothing objectionable in that.

I would watch every time the storytellers circle formed, and oh, how I longed to understand what was being said! How I yearned to sit myself near the guild members and listen to what they were sharing. I did not know, you see, that the guild members communicated in the language of the Authorities; our cook spoke her own language, and so I assumed the Guild did, too, and was too aware of my differences to dare approach closely enough to hear anything, and I hung back, feeling unwelcome.

Our cook, whose registered name was Mary, treated me exactly as she treated the other children who seemed as attracted to the back door of our kitchen as I was to the storytelling circle, and when she assigned them little chores to do, she always found one for me; and when she rewarded them for their work with meals made of leftovers from the food served the customers, she would give me my own bowl, and send me off to sit in the dust behind the inn with the children of the People.

In an amazingly short period of time I learned to join those children, and we told our jokes in the language of the

Authorities, sometimes using a few words of the language of the People, and my mother often laughed and said my father would probably shit in his own hat if he could hear me, my accent not only what he would call 'provincial' but actually heavy enough to be called 'Coy,' and all my mother did toward forcing any kind of an education upon me was teach me to read and write, and teach me how to use the learning tapes if I was interested.

I was interested. And one day, playing with the Coys, I said something that sparked their interest; they wanted to know where I had learned such a thing. And so it was we all began to 'play' with the learning tapes, not regularly, not every day, not starting at a certain hour and working until another certain hour, but whenever we felt we needed to find out something. For example, one day we saw a freight convoy, and we hid, staring with a mix of fear and fascination as the huge machines crawled on tracks across the face of the Mother, cutting the grass in regular strips, leaving precise raw gouges in her face, and we had no idea what it was we were seeing. So, as soon as it felt safe, we went back to the Inn and started entering questions in the machine, and that is how we learned about track machines and tons of supplies and the strange Authority men who are the Convoyers. Out of this curiosity, several of us began to ask questions about the power that moves the track machines, and others wanted to know how a record was kept of which freight was sent where.

None of that interested me at all. My fascination was still with the storytelling Guild, and often the Coys would be playing with my machine and I would be watching hungrily as the Guild came together. And one day, my courage fragile but at least present, I moved closely enough to realize I could understand every word being said!

That day has assumed more importance than my birthday. I sat politely distant, from then on, and listened, and one day our Cook, Mary, said there were members of the Guild who had wondered to her why it was a child was being taught she was superior to other people. Did I think I was too good to sit in the listener's circle? Did I object to sitting beside the People? And when I told Mary I was afraid someone would tell me to leave, because of my skin color and my hair and eyes and such, Mary gave me a look of such total disbelief I knew I had misunderstood almost everything ever demonstrated to me.

So I moved into the listener's circle, and thought I had died and gone to that Other Place. I would listen, and more importantly, I would watch, the hand movements, the facial expressions, and I began to recognize which of the tellers was from our village and which from nearby, which was from the Outlands, which was once made to attend a residential school, which had been raised by the Outcasts, which had come early or late to the Guild.

I check every day, and on those days when there was no circle, I had a life like any other child. But if a Guild member arrived with her armband displayed, she no more than settled her backside in the dust of the central compound than I was there, with water, and with food, with meat and fruit and whatever I could sleaze from Mary, and I would put it where the Guild member could find it, then hunker myself down and wait.

One day, four Guild members came together, and one member had the accent of a one who had attended residential school, one had the manners of an Outcast, and two I could not place, for at first they did not recount any stories. I felt as if other people knew something that day that I did not. No more did those four women settle themselves, and drink of the juice I had brought, eat of the food I had managed to sleaze, than the two began to tell stories. First one, and then the other, with hardly any pause between stories. One would tell a story, then look at me, and there would be the space of perhaps four breaths, and the other would tell a story, and then, she, too, would look at me. And there were so many people in the Listener's circle! I had never seen so many people, some sitting, some hunkering, some standing, and even Mary had taken her place, and most of the Coy children I knew, and still it would be a story, and a pause, and a story, and a pause. And I see some of you are smiling, and probably you are wondering

14

at my stupidity, but I had only partly learned some of what had been demonstrated to me.

Then, suddenly, one of the quiet women looked at me and all storytelling stopped. Nothing but silence. And she reached for the juice jug and drank of it, then took a small morsel of food and ate it. Then drank again, and then, she spoke directly to me.

I had never before heard an accent like hers. As soon as she spoke I knew I was listening to what my Coy friends called "the soft tongue." Often they had said their grandmother had spoken in the soft tongue, or their Aunt still spoke the soft tongue at family meetings. And by everything that was 'logical' I ought not to have understood a word, but I understood. Not everything. But enough. And I knew she was saying I had brought juice for her throat and food for her belly, that I had fed her body, but what did I bring for her spirit? I stared. I had nothing to offer. She persisted, saying that the spirit needed nourishment even more than the body, for a person can go days without water, weeks without food, but only hours without hope, or love. And what did I have for her soul?

I felt tears on my face. I did not know what she wanted. And then the fourth woman spoke, and she spoke in the language of the Authorities, but with that deep soft accent of the ones whose first language is the soft language. And she said, and I remember her words exactly, she said "Tell me how you came to be who you are."

I nearly ran away! Then I felt someone sit directly behind me and put her hands on my shoulders, and when I turned, Mary, our Cook, was behind me, and she just smiled and nodded and told me to repeat what I had been telling her in the kitchen.

Long ago, I said to them, Long ago and far away in that Other Place which is home to the Authorities, long before there were Authorities, there were people. And these people were very small, slender, with dark hair and dark skin, and they lived in little homes dug into the hillsides, and their walls shored up the hillside and kept it from tumbling in on them, and the smoke from their cooking fires went up to a hole through the dirt and rose from the hills as if the hills themselves were breathing. And these people lived in families, with the oldest mother as their wise one, and everything belonged to the women, and all women were mother to all children. A daughter seldom left the home of her mother, and if a young man took her fancy, he would move in with her and stay with her, and if they had good fortune, he would be father of her children. When the little home grew too small for the number of children, the men would enlarge it, adding rooms, until the hills were tunnelled, and the faint blue smoke hung in the air. And usually a woman and a man would stay together all the days of their lives, but if a man got sick and died, or if he had an accident and died, or if he was not content and left, or if he offended the woman in any way, then he would leave, with those things that were his, and the woman and her children would stay where they belonged, and she might live alone, or she might take a fancy to another man.

In the soft days of first spring, the little people would go to their fields and would dance in them, and would plant barley seed, and they would spread the contents of their compost holes, and then, between the rows of planted barley seed, they would couple happily, encouraging the fertility of the fields, and the fertility of the women, and the barley grew strong and rich. They took their animals to the grasslands and there were people who stayed with the animals, collecting their droppings, and every so often this, too, would be taken to the barley fields and placed between the sprouts. And with the barley they made cakes, and bread, and brewed barley beer, and made barley soup, and there were other things they gathered and gleaned in the growing time. And when it was time, they would harvest the barley, and gently turn the soil, and put it to sleep for the winter, then, with their food stored, they would retire to their little houses and spend the cold silence of winter in dreaming and in discussing their dreams, in talking, in singing, in the learning of musical instruments.

And all was well. Until one day Strangers arrived. Tall, fair-haired, strange eyed and fierce. They brought beasts and animals unlike those of the people and turned them loose in the grasslands, and they saw the fields of barley, and harvested it for themselves. They cared nothing for the little people, and, in fact, thought them scarcely human. The suffering of the little people was extreme. And all winter, it got worse, until they were forced to eat the bitter wild herbs and even the grass, which only re-enforced the opinion of the Strangers, and was used as proof that the little people were different, and less.

Children died of hunger in a land that had never known hunger. The old ones took themselves away from the meager shelter of the empty little homes in the earth, and they lay themselves down in the snow and ice, and died, that there be more of what little they had, more for the children, who are always the future.

A woman of the little people watched her daughter sicken for lack of milk, and knew her scrawny infant was doomed. In desperation, she took the skinny dark baby and crept to the village the Strangers had built. She found a window not locked, and went into a house, and in that house, she found the fat, healthy, sleeping blond son of a Stranger. She took him from his warm bed, and left in his stead her own half-starved child, and then she returned to her cheerless little house, and she took the child of the Strangers with her, as hostage.

In the morning the Stranger woman found the changeling child and she screamed with sorrow and grief. Of course, search parties went out looking for the child and whoever it was who had stolen him, but they found no trace to follow, and the woman knew in her heart that if she killed this changeling, or neglected it and let it die, her own beloved child would perish.

It was easy to see from the dark infant's condition that there was little or no food among the little people. And the poor mother, though she was a Stranger, could not stand the thought of her son starving. Every night she left food out, in the hope it would be given to her son. Every morning, the milk was gone, the food was gone, and the woman continued to hope.

The dark changeling daughter grew fat, and learned to walk,

and to laugh, and then she learned to talk, and the language she learned was the language of the Strangers. And when she learned to say "Mother" she said it to the healthy blond Stranger woman. Who called the dark changeling child "daughter."

And other fat blond children were taken, and other skinny dark little ones were left in their place, and soon the Strangers realized that what they did to the little people, they did to their own flesh and blood, and the horrors were less and less. The dark little people also learned that hiding in holes in the hillside is no way to ensure survival, and they showed themselves, and bit by bit, little by little, the two people began to share the land. And in time, a dark child married a blond child, and they had children, and life went on in a new and different way that, over the generations, began to seem like the only way it had ever been.

But one day Invaders arrived, and they looked different, and talked different, and their god was different, and they took the land and made it theirs, they took the animals and called them their own, and they oppressed the ones who had always lived there, and enslaved them, and sent them down into mines to dig the coal, which the Invaders sold in foreign lands and shipped off in boats commanded by their own officers, but worked by the people who were the many times great grandchildren of the little people and the Strangers. And life was miserable.

Other Invaders began to envy the richness that resulted from the mines and from the labor of the poor slaves, and they came in a great armada, and the Invaders met them in battle. The poor people, the poor sad miserable bastards, took the day off from toiling in the mines and sat on the cliffs and watched the slaughter and celebrated, for all the Invaders were killing all the other Invaders, and to the poor sad miserable bastards, one Invader looks and sounds and acts like another and the wars of the rich are no business of the poor.

But then they noticed that in the ships of the invading armada, there were people like themselves, only darker, with tight curly hair, and these poor sad buggers were chained to the oars of the huge ships, so that when the ship was damaged, the officers and rich could attempt to flee but the poor were stuck, and if the ship went under the water, these poor buggers were drowned. And from these poor black buggers came the sound of many hearts breaking, a sound that carried over the water to the ears of the poor sad miserable bastards on the cliffs and their own hearts began to break, and they could no longer just sit there like lumps, but ran down the cliffs to the beach, and pushed their little boats into the water, and rowed out to the damaged ships, and dared to clamber up and free as many of the poor black buggers as they could, and the oppressed took the chains from the oppressed, the slaves freed other slaves, and all the poor buggers and sad bastards healed their broken hearts as best they could, and made it safe back to shore, except for those who perished, and they all went off together, and the result of it all was that the rich killed off so many of the rich there weren't enough of them to oppress the poor any more, and the sad bastards and poor buggers reclaimed the land, and lived together and sang together and even loved together, and their children were free.

For generations they were free and then the Conquerors came, and you can imagine how that went, the same thing all over again, and the poor buggers and sad bastards and poor suffered terribly, and their children were taken from them and their language denied them, their religion was attacked and their culture was trampled and they, themselves, were enslaved.

And, as before, a child of the Conquerors saw a child of the poor, and there was love, in spite of all, and things began to follow the same path, except that, this time, the Conquerors wanted more land, and to have it, they moved against the poor and burned their crofts and shaelings, and rounded them up with armies, and crammed them on transports, and sailed them over the very edge of the world to a place nobody had seen before, and they left them there, with only what little they had, and nobody cared if the poor survived or died, except, of course, the poor, and who ever listens to them?

In the new land, the poor managed to cling to life, managed to endure, and they built a few homes, and tilled some fields, and hunted animals for food and began to establish themselves. Only to discover there were people already living in that land! People who looked absolutely different from these poor abandoned fools, people who considered these abandoned suffering poor to be Conquerors and Invaders and Strangers, and there was much turmoil, with some of the children of the Dispossessed becoming exactly what the dark haired Originals thought them to be, becoming Conquerors and Invaders and right bastards, but others, often the brothers and sisters of the right bastards, remembering the stories of persecution in the homeland, and not wanting to do to the Originals what had been done to them, and in time, these ones and their children learned to live with the children of the Originals, and things continued.

Except that the right bastards were still there, still being right bastards, and they moved to send the Mixed and the Sociable and the Sharing and the others right off that world altogether, over the very rim of the sky, and they sent the bureaucrats and supervisors along to be sure that everyone behaved as the law said they ought and so it was that we arrived here and found that here, again, we are Outlanders, Outworlders, Foreigners, and considered to be assholes, by the Coys and the Authorities both, for the Authorities are those who follow the Right Bastards who grew to power because of the Conquerors who had followed the Invaders who replaced the Strangers who had tried to destroy the language and culture, the religion and history of the poor buggers and sad bastards.

None of this has been on any of the learning tapes, and none of this has been verifiable with the machine; I have tried to find out about this any number of times, and can find nothing. This story has been told me often by my mother, and she says it will never be in the tapes, not in History or Anthropology or anything because the Right Bastards do not want this story told, nor do they want any of the other stories told, and so they will not program the tapes nor in any way help spread the story. My mother says they even try to erase the story, and that they have a million ways to attempt to smother it, from laughter to scorn to medication and even surgical altering of memory, and my mother says they will all shit in all their hats when they realize the story is still alive and well and living in the minds and hearts of so many.

And when I had finished telling the story my mother had given me there was a long silence in the crowd, and among the four women of the Guild. And then the one who had spoken to me asking what it was I had brought as food and drink for her soul, reached out and took my hand, and tugged gently. And Mary lifted me from my backside in the dust, and pushed gently, and with no understanding of what was happening I found myself standing in the storytellers circle. And Mary pushed down on my shoulders, and I put my backside in the dust again, and sat in the circle of storytellers, and when they tied the cloth around my arm, the cloth that shows me as an apprentice in the Guild, I sobbed aloud, and felt as if my heart would burst with joy. And yes, I am of The Others, and yes my eyes are a different shape and a different color, and yes my hair is not the same as the hair of the People, but we know this land as our Mother and we know the taste of her water, we know her kiss on our cheeks each time the breeze blows, and we know there are wrongs which must be righted, wrongs which will be righted, and which we will right with our stories, and with the love with which we feed each others' souls. And though it is true my father is probably even now shitting in his own hat, it is also true my mother provides food and drink and a place to stay free of charge for all Guild members, and that sometimes, when we are very lucky, she sits quietly, with her hands folded in her lap, and she sings in that soft language accent of her own people, sings songs of the crofts and the shaellings, sings songs of the green valleys of that homeland she has never seen, and she sings of the things our songsters sing; of hope and love and sorrow and pain and peace and joy and again, love.

Third

When I was eight or nine—or maybe ten or eleven—I don't remember for sure, now, Klopinum would share her stories with me. My mom was working as an aide in the white hospital at the top of the hill, where black-haired kids with eyes like sad holes burned in wool blankets stared through windows at the rolling fields their TB lungs would not allow them to run in, or to jump or yell in, or to chase in, or ride bikes in, or do any of the things kids were intended by creation to do.

You be good, now, my mom would say, and off she'd go, leaving her own kids at home and walking a mile or so to the job that provided money that bought the food that kept us healthy and sometimes, especially when she was on afternoon shift, I'd half waken and she'd be standing by my bed, looking down at me, her eyes glistening slightly, glistening damply in the past-midnight dark.

She had a real thing about those forms they sent home from school, she'd always sign, and they'd jab us in the arm with all this stuff they said would keep us from getting sick. Didn't matter if it was smallpox, typhoid, diptheria, she didn't even look at the form, she signed, and we got stuck in the arm, but we didn't get any of those sicknesses, and we didn't get TB, either, and she'd tell us Stop Complaining, the kids where I work would give anything to be able to do even half what it is you can do. Not much we could say to that, just roll up the sleeve and get jabbed again.

Anyway, she'd go off to work, and I'd feed those few scraggly hens I had in a cage under the steps against the front of the house, safe from the neighbor's dog. One of my first abortive attempts at capitalism, and probably the reason I am sympathetic toward farmers today. Fill their water, gather the occasional grudgingly given egg, take it in the house and wash off the feathers and chickenshit and who knows what, then clean the sink, wash the dishes, clean the sink again, and the day was mine.

Get the red CCM from where it was leaning against the outside wall, start running with it, pushing it alongside me, then, then, then, when everything felt Just Right, jump up on the seat, as close as I could get to the running starts the cowboys took in the Saturday matinee. Even then I wondered how often they fell off before they learned how to do it. I'd lost yards of skin before I could plop my fanny on the leather-covered seat.

Down the camp road to Fifth street, then straight down Fifth all the way to where it turned into Pine street. (And why two names for one street? Nobody ever explained.) To the highway, turn left, then turn right, down over the tracks to the reserve, past the big building they called the Band Office, and you could see the whitepainted church off to your right, standing in a field of grass in the summerholiday sunshine.

Down to the street that ran parallel to the beach; it had no name then, god knows if it has one now.

Dogs, everywhere. With and without puppies trailing behind, some friendly, some waiting for a chance to rip your flesh, they'd run and boil around in the soft dust of the road, yapping and barking, almost upsetting the bike until someone would holler and then the whole lot would scoot off in search of some other entertainment. Kids yelled, or waved, or grinned, or ignored me, and adults sat on the steps or porches, with men in dark pants and undershirts, the women in cotton dresses, the old women with kerchiefs over their heads, tied at the back of their necks, the kids, like me, in old clothes, play clothes we called them, to distinguish them from school clothes which had to be kept clean.

They sat on the steps or porches and the open doors to the houses gaped darkly, even in broad daylight, and nobody ever seemed in a rush. Oh, once in a while you'd see some guy draped over a fencepost or on his knees by a ditch, puking his guts out, drunk, and a lot of the kids had marks like the kind I wore a lot, those hot red blotches where the old man's hand connected with a good one, or those thin fire strips where his belt had cracked sharply. But mostly, the people seemed pretty passive, and content.

For years I didn't even know what Klopinum's name was, if

23

she'd ever told me, I'd forgotten it. I just called her "Auntie." If anyone else came to visit while I was there, Klopinum would tell them my name and then add "Her momma works at our hospital," and whoever it was would look at me, then smile, as if I had just been forgiven something that wasn't my fault anyway. Once, twenty-five years later, in Alert Bay, on hearing my name, someone, a fisherman who sang Country and Western, asked "Where you from?" and I said "Nanaimo" and he asked if I was related to the woman with the same name who had worked at the Indian hospital. "She's my mom," I said, and right then and there I had to go to his house, meet his wife and kids, and out came the photo album, and there was my mom, magically young again, standing by a whitepainted metal crib, her arm around a boy of five or six, both of them smiling. And another picture, the same boy in pajamas, sitting grinning from ear to ear at a small table, and on the table, presents, and a birthday cake with candles, and my mom, laughing, ready to help him blow out his candles. "She was like my own mom when I didn't have one," he said, and his wife told me to stay for supper. Before the meal was over there were brothers and sisters and an uncle and a few aunts, telling me to please tell my mom thank you for being so nice to Sonny, and when I got home and told her, out came her photo album, and there was Sonny, a boy again, with my mom, and even a picture of him in his new clothes, hugging my mom and looking scared shitless. In the background the strangers who were his family, waiting to take him to the home he couldn't remember, back to Alert Bay.

Sometimes we'd just walk along the edge of the water on the lip of dampness where the spindrift had dried and crackled under our feet with the stiff sun-withered seaweed. Sometimes we followed the path into the bush, stepping from hot sunlight to shaded dampness, our feet squishing in the underlay, sending up scents and smells and tastes it took me years to rediscover.

Look she'd say, yella vi'lets, smell, she'd say, thimbleberry leaves. Here, she'd say, chew this, and when I did it tasted like licorice.

Sometimes we didn't talk at all, other times we both yapped and chattered.

But the best times were the times Klopinum told me stories. Hear that, she'd say. Old Raven sitting up in a dead snag minding everybody else's business. Hear her? Bossing and scolding and giving advice nobody wants to hear. That Raven ... and she'd smile and there'd be a story. Raven is the trickster, she fools and is fooled, and her voice is a sharp stone that breaks the day. One day, Raven....

Sit on this log, she'd say, and let's us watch Snipe working for her dinner. You never see Snipe wasting her time. But if you watch her long enough you'll see that even though she's working all the time, she's having fun, too. Hear her talk, talk, talk, talkin to her fam'ly? Hear them talk talk talkin right back? Every one of em busy busy busy and havin a good time.

Oh, Eagle, she shrugged, what's so great about an eagle, just a big garbage truck is what Eagle is. Just another kind of sea gull except she can't swim like Gull does. Now if you want a bird, you look at Osprey. She never eats somethin been dead in the sun, never eats somethin she didn't catch fresh herself, you don't see Osprey chewin away on spawn dead salmon.

Here, you twists the heads off like this, see. Peel 'em down between the legs, like so ... I'll show you one more time then you can do your own. And the prawns, pink with red stripes, still steaming from the boiling sea water, dumped in the colander to drain, filled the room with scent. We took them out onto the porch and shelled them all, ate a few dipped in butter, ate a few more, then more until not one single morsel more would have fit inside us. All the small ones, she said, are boys, and all the big ones are female. See how they carry their eggs up against them, between their legs, caught on those little hair-things. The eggs are the best part, but hard to get at, you have to suck and nibble and make all kinds of noise. They all start off the same, all start off to be boys, then, when they're big enough, they change. Prawn has to be smart to get big, and only the smart ones have eggs to turn into baby prawns. The dumb ones are food for the fish. Dogfish are like that, too, start off as males, all the small, fast ones, all males, then, when they're old enough, and big enough, and wise, they change. Big female breeds with a small fast male, maybe only one time every four, five years. Don't know how they manage that. Magic, I guess. The world is full of magic. It's everywhere.

Dogfish breeds but she doesn't have a whole bunch eggs at one time. Not like, say, frog, or salmon. Or most other things. Dogfish, her babies come like blackberries, there's never a bush covered with ripe ones, you ever notice that? Some green, some pink, some red, some maroon, some black, and a dogfish, if you catch a female and open'er up, she has one baby that's all set to be born, you can put it in water and off it'll go, just a bit of egg sac left. And another almost as big but not quite, it might be able to swim, might not, got more egg in the sac, slowing it down, still feeding it. And one a bit smaller yet, and another even smaller right down to where it's just an egg with a little black dot in it, and every couple days Dogfish has another baby. Magic. Lots of magic.

Green eyes, dogfish has, and they shine like there's a light burning in her head, soon as she dies the light goes out, you know the second she's gone over, just like that, the light is gone. Makes me cry.

Toads eyes, now, they're gold, and sort split, like, hard to describe. You look at a toad and you feel funny inside yourself. Sometimes people think toads are ugly, mud colored, lumpy, some say you get warts from toads but I never did. But if you pick her up and *look* at her you'll see some Magic. First off, how she feels. Smooth. Looks lumpy and rough, feels smooth like silk. White belly, with little spots and most of the time she'll pee on your hand; that's very good luck. Very good luck I tell you. And she smiles all the time. Her whole mouth is one big smile, night and day. When it starts to get cold, toad, she finds her a nice place, under a windfall log or in a sand bank or some place private. I got one lives under my house! That's why this place always has such a good feel to it. Colder it gets, sleepier toad gets, and sometimes, I start diggin my garden early, maybe to put seaweed on it or somethin and I dig me up a toad, sleeping in the dirt. If I do that, I make a hole with my hand and put her right back again, apologize to her for maybe disturbing her sleep. What she does, see, is send her spirit out of her body to a warm place, so her body sleeps and her spirit plays. Most times when the spirit outs like that, you don't dare even touch the person or thing or you break the connection and the spirit can't ever return and the body dies. But toad? You can move her to a whole other place and she can find herSelf just fine. Soon as it gets warm she starts to wake up, and when the spring rains soak everything, you'll hear burump burump, and soon, toad'll be back out again, with her white belly and big smile and gold jewel eyes. I never seen jewels as pretty. I stood lots of times in front of the jewel store and stared at rubies and emeralds and di'monds, and I never saw anything as pretty as toad's eyes. Tiger eye stone is almost as nice, but not really. Oh, there's magic in this world I tell you.

Klopinum wasn't much taller than I was, her body a round sturdy barrel. She wore brown lisle stockings and low-heeled shoes, a clean housedress with an apron over top, with pockets full of treasures. Her hair was going from gray to white, no butter-yellow streaks in it like some, and she kept it loosely pinned in a bun at the nape of her neck, it escaped often and wisped softly around her face, as fine and as difficult to manage as baby hair. Her chubby short-fingered Salish hands would reach back, the hair would tumble loose briefly, new-chick fine, then, fingers flashing, she would do magic and the bun would be back, not a hairpin to be seen; magic, the world is full of magic. There, that's better, she would laugh, that hair's gonna drive me crazy one day.

I knew about hair like that. Early memories of tsk tsk such flyaway hair, of barrettes sliding out, of bobby pins clicking to the floor, of hair ribbons lost Heaven knew where, and of hair blowing in the breeze, getting in my mouth, my eyes, and finally they said Oh, it's a mess, and started braiding it, pulling the pigtails so tight the skin around my eyes was stretched taut as a drum hide, my eyes made even more slanty, and the more I protested the harder they tugged. Gonna drive me crazy one day I mutterd but only Klopinum knew the meaning of the words. Everyone else in my family had dark hair, thick and manageable, and some, the lucky ones, had curly hair, a few even had hair that was almost kinkycurly but mine was blond and no more curl to it than to swamp grass.

Klopinum had a round flat face, her eyes almost lost in folds, wrinkles, creases, lines, and her forehead was so prominent her eyes seemed hidden under the shelf of her brow. Her hands were gnarled, knuckles swollen from hours of picking oysters in cold water, digging clams in frigid mud flats, her skin was wrinkled beyond description, and she ought to have been long past the age of running, ought to have been past the time of life to jump a beach log or clamber up a pile of rocks, but she did all that, and more. Laughing. People forget how to live, they forgot a whole bunch stuff, you want a good strong body you got to teach it what you want it to do otherwise you wind up livin in an old wreck, not able to go nowhere nobody'd want to go. Don't tighten up when you run, you just run, loose, and breathe like a dog. You lungs go all the way down to your bellybutton, so don't breathe with your chest, breathe with your belly, and when you got a bad cold, sniff warm sea water up your nose and wash out all the germs, it'll hurt you, but not as bad as being sick.

Bellybutton, she'd tease, poking me, you got an in-one or an out-one? Mine's an in-one she told me. Mine, too, I admitted.

You keep that bellybutton covered in the wintertime, there's no fat on the inside of it, the cold will get to your innards and you'll get sick. Everyone was so convinced we were up to our ears in sickness, everyone was waiting for death, certain it hid behind every rock, waiting to reach out and grab a kid and break everyone's heart. You gotta know, she told me, you gotta Know you're precious. You're a child. Children are precious. Oh God, we lost so many, and for a while I didn't know her, she wasn't my Auntie, she was someone else, and the light had faded, her spirit had gone somewhere else. And then she was back again, and hugging me, making me promise I would be careful and not get sick.

My mother with her innoculations and dentists
Klopinum with her sea water and dried roots
My grandmother with her north English spring tonic and mustard plasters
Eat salmonberries, they're good for you, the first berries, they'll clean the winter out of your bowels and you won't get sick
And I knew she loved me.

She had blackberry tarts, I remember that, so it was probably August and the summer so hot and still the dust hung in the air, the heat waves shimmered above the surface of the sea.

Klopinum's fingers were stained blue with berry juice and her feet stuck out straight in front of her. We were sitting on the sand, leaning against a weather-bleached log, her shoes, I remember, were canvas sneakers, gray now, and almost finished.

Most of her stories I'd heard four or five or a dozen times, and could recite word for word with her. You tell a good story, she told me sometimes, and laughed happily. But that day she told me a story for the first time, and then never told me it again, although I asked for it often enough. You'll remember it on your own, she answered, when it's time. You heard it when I told you, you know that story even if you don't know you know it, and when it's time, you'll remember. You don't need me ever again to tell you that story.

She told me of the Creator. Not a man and not a woman but neither, and both, it doesn't matter. And the Creator is the Creator and is The Voice Which Must Be Obeyed. A good force, a good spirit, a good soul. Made everything in this world and all the other worlds, made the birds and fish and animals and trees and plants and rocks and us. Made it all. And when everything was done and everyone was alive, the clouds and rocks and sky and ocean and fish and earth and animals and people and everything you ever saw or didn't see, when we were all alive and the job all done, the Creator smiled. And knew that nobody that lived would ever know everything or have all the answers, but everybody would always have questions, and so Creator took a little bit of the best of everything and with it, Creator made a river, and hid that river in everything. It's in me and it's in you and it's in that cedar tree and it's in that rock and it's in every grain of sand on this beach and every drop of rain that ever fell or will fall, and in sunshine and cloud, in chickens and osprey, in beauty and ugliness, in dogs 'n' cats and in huckleberries and spawning salmon. It's a river of Copper, because Copper is sacred, comes in five colors and that's one more than magic four. And all the holy people, all the sacred people, all the special people who have gifts are part of this river. The poets and painters and carvers and singers and dancers and drummers and storytellers and everybody that walks and talks and breathes and lives or who ever did. The dead we love are part of this river and the ones who haven't come into this world are part of this river, and if you have love, and faith, and courage and trust, even when you're afraid, you can find that river and go to it and drink Truth from it and find some answers for yourself.

You should write a book, I told her. I had always been excited by books. You could write a book and people would buy it and read the stories and it would be wonderful! Everybody would know your stories.

No. Klopinum looked away, and for a while didn't look or feel or sound like my Auntie at all, just an old woman with tired eyes, like when she'd talked of kids being taken sick. Not me. Nobody wants those stories. She shrugged, then smiled, and finally laughed. I'm just an old klooch, she said. Who listens? Anyway, I can't read and I can't write, I never went to school and writers go to universities. No. I'm just an old klooch.

You could tell them, and get someone else to do the writing, I insisted, as stubborn as anyone is at that age. She looked at me, and kissed me, and smiled again, and then reached out her blackberry stained fingers, took my hand in hers and patted it. Tell you what, she said, I'll give them stories to you. They're yours, now.

When I was eleven I told my mother I was going to be a writer. When I was fifteen and she was still working long hours for low pay and there were by then four kids to feed instead of two, and money was scarcer than ever, she managed, god knows how, to buy me a typewriter. You can't be a writer without one she said.

Magic, the world is full of magic. It's everywhere....

Magic around us, in front of us, behind us, beneath us, above us, and in us, magic everywhere and the evidence of our own eyes proves it.

My hair, dandelion fluff, unruly, wisping out even from pigtails, darkened steadily, and by age twenty-one there was little evidence it had once been so blond as to be white. It defied curlers, and pin curls and even home permanents, it sulked under setting gel and waited under Dippity-Doo, and the pigtails were too childish so became one long braid, down my back. An East Indian woman from the Punjab taught me how to train the end of the braid so I didn't have to use an elastic, and my children knew me throughout their lives as a woman with long hair.

And the dominant ideology cut the forests and opened mines, they laid blacktop across the face of the island and altered forever the foreshore and beaches, they built sawmills and pulp mills and spotted the sea with booming grounds and drove bulldozers through spawning streams and spilled diesel in lakes, they clear-cut and forgot to reforest, they shipped raw logs to Japan, they sprayed poison and spread chemical fertilizers, they scattered pesticide and fungicide and the osprey grew fewer, the eagles almost vanished, the heron became a picture in a book instead of a regular sight on the clean beaches, and the sea birds died covered with oil spilled from tankers. The sky was stained with black smoke, gray smoke, white smoke, the strawberry fields were covered with subdivisions, the holly bushes ripped out and replaced with hydro poles, the lakes once teeming with trout were almost empty, and we wrote our letters and held our demonstrations, we presented briefs to the government and tried to be logical and the devastation spread. Klopinum was gone and I was frightened, and we appealed to the law, to the church, to anyone anywhere who might possibly listen.

The Haida took it to court, presented their land claims and blockaded the logging road, and we hoped, we prayed, we waited, and the court turned the Haida down; and I knew, I was going to cut off my braid. Cutting off your braid can be a sign of mourning or a sign of defiance, it can be a sign of anger, or it can be a sign of determination. The shaman/dancer asked me why I was asking him to cut my braid. I said To show there is no limit to what we will give to protect the mother. To show we will talk, or not talk, we will demonstrate or not demonstrate, we will try politics if we have to, we will give everything, even the hair on our head, but we will not quietly allow the disrespect to continue, for she is our Mother and we are no longer infants and thus allowed to be irresponsible, we are adults and it is time to force the changes. If we must give our money, we will give our money, if we must give our lives, we will give our lives, if we must give our fingernail parings and our hair, we will give that, but we will no longer not protest this madness.

My braid hung to my backside, I could sit on it, and we washed it according to custom, the shaman braided it the special way and bound it in the special fashion, and he prayed and taught me a prayer, then with a knife never before used for anything, a knife he had prayed over and sought a vision about, he cut off my braid right above where my collar would be, and then he prayed, and we wept, he wrapped it, and took it with him.

My children had never seen me with short hair, and they stared. One daughter wept and had to leave the room.

The next day I got up and went into the kitchen for a cup of coffee and my adopted Haida daughter stared at me. Stared and stared. Then went to get her sister, my blond daughter who had wept, and when she came into the kitchen she stared and stared.

I went to the bathroom expecting to find I had grown another nose or a third ear. The face reflected in the mirror was my face, my same old face, lined now, with wrinkles around the eyes and lines where my smile fits. And the hair on my head was curly.

I wear my hair short, now, and expect I will until land claims are met with justice, morality, and respect. And they will be met with justice, morality and respect, it is inevitable, the proof is on my head, the evidence of our eyes is there for the world to see, the evidence of magic; in a world full of magic injustice cannot prevail, and this world is full of magic, magic is everywhere....

In The Beginning
There Was Humming

DEENA METZGER

*I*n the beginning there was humming. There was humming
from one end of the universe to the other, even across the
sacred river, there was only humming and the sacred river, it
was also a song. So there was no separation between the
worlds, there was only one world in the hum, except for the
cadences and the rising and falling except as the hum altered in
its humming. The hum changed from moment to moment but
it was always the same and it was always singing.

And one day, though there was neither day nor night, there
was neither yesterday nor tomorrow, when the hum was singing to itself, when it was nothing but humming, there was coming to meet it, another hum, out of nothingness. One hum filling the universe in the one direction and another hum filling
the universe in the one direction, each hum called in response
to the other out of nothingness, unable to resist the song. The
hums met in the middle of themselves where they were quiver-
ing and they turned about each other, each one singing, and
each one a song, and each exactly like the other and each totally distinct from the other. And where they met, from the
vibrant impact of their meeting, two hums as if they were one
became not one hum but one hum condensed into one note and

that note trembling until it shattered. And from then on there was humming and there was also listening, one hum became two from that explosion.

And listening was a great light and a great darkness and a great fire and they twisted, humming, about the fire, becoming one note and each time broken again, also into a mist and one end of the mist falling into water and the other end of the mist rising to be wind. In one moment they had been the same and now without changing, for they were the same, they were also altered and different. In one moment they had been one point of humming and now they were broken, were also time and space, were water and wind. In the beginning there had been nothingness, there was nothing but beginning and now also there was a great fire.

It was exactly as it had been in the beginning and also it was the world. So in the beginning there was humming and the humming became longing and the longing had been one hum in one voice and then it became also one longing with many voices. The hum and the longing were the same and the hum was also not longing. Now in the beginning for the first time there was so much in the world, so much that was different, also so many voices, they were lonely. When they were one hum, when there was one hum, there could have been no loneliness and now nothing had changed, for nothing can change, but still they were also broken into pieces.

They sang to each other, one singing and the other listening and then the other singing and the one listening and the singing and listening wrapped itself into a moving braid of longing, it was alive as they bent about each other. The braid was the live humming translated into a great light both still and moving. They sang together, or they hummed each in their own cadence; they were stopping and starting, they were shining, they were beginning to breathe. It was music.

In the beginning, then, there was music. First there was humming and then there was music. The humming by itself could not be music. The music like the humming went on for a long time, forever, from the beginning. And there was great beauty in the music.

But for all the beauty in the music, there was still longing and they were lonely. Once there had been one hum and no loneliness and then they were two and they were shattered. They brought their brokenness together, but it was only notes, and they could not join them. They could only sing them, one and then the other, or together, but they remained two notes or a thousand or a great fire and light or a mist and a wind or time and space.

So even as they had hummed together so they began to hum apart, to withdraw from each other. As they had been drawn together so they pulled apart in their humming to the far ends of the universe to the edge of nothing from which they had come, they pulled their hums after them so that the song became fainter and fainter and the pulses of the universe barely audible; it was almost winter and from the ends of the universe they hummed and hummed, it was very still now, there was silence.

In the beginning there was silence and it lasted a long time, it lasted forever from the beginning. There were two hums and they were absolutely silent. They did not want to be two hums so far from their edge of silence and nothingness, so from their silence, from the edge of nothingness, they began to create one great hum at the same time so that it would implode from two directions in the same moment with such force and heat that it would fuse them and they would be one again, only one hum singing, as it had been in the beginning and still was. And no other hum coming out of nothingness.

And so from a whisper of a hum in the silence on the edge of nothingness, began humming, and increased in speed and pitch and intensity until the one humming, two hums, met violently, the entire universe pitching and weaving and vibrant and the two hums meeting as one imploding as they hoped into one, and it was not music, as they feared, but meeting as one. There was nothing else for awhile, forever, there was nothing else but the two hums as one, inseparable and indistinct from each other. And it was humming, a great implosion of humming, it was one hum they were humming and the humming heaved in them and they could not contain it, it was the point of humming, and they held it forever, from the beginning.

Then it came to pass as it must when nothing changes and everything must change, there was a longing for silence and they could not hold the humming but had to explode again, to be broken again, to be two so there could be one, separation and unity,motion and stillness, so there could be both humming and silence. They went toward their brokenness as joyfully and with as much longing and need and sorrow as they had gone toward their pointedness. And it was not music this time coming from their brokenness, it was a louder humming, it was dancing. Now there was humming and breaking which was dancing and the hums formed a great dancing braid of light and the strands were misty and shining, they were time and space, they were water and wind, they were night and darkness, they were even the serpent and the tree, they were the moon and the sun, they were even darkness and light, they were even women and men. Even this one hum could not remain what it was, it erupted as it touched, even as they touched and became one — so they touched and were imploded and they touched and were exploded and broken and made one. From the beginning, forever. It was a long dance, as long as humming, it lasted forever from the beginning. They could not contain it or themselves. It did not stop and it could not continue.

There had been humming, and humming became water and wind, or time and space, or music and then there was humming again and it became serpent and tree, darkness and light, it was dancing and from it from the midst of the music and the dancing, from the hum and the humming, came earth, it came out of them like a great luminous egg, it was a stone, breathing, it came out of them, jointly, it was the image of their dance in colors, and it turned, for they had been turning, about the great light moon and sun as they had been singing the great light into being.

And so it was from the beginning when men and women were apart they hummed to each other to create their loneliness, which they loved—it was song and it brought them together—which they loved—and it was dancing. So it was from the beginning there was always music and there was always dancing, always separate and always together, and after that, from the beginning there was always only stillness and only humming, an only hum; it was sufficient.

And because they wanted the people to remember, for without remembering they were only as particles of water or pieces of wind, for like the hum, the people were all remembering, for this they gave them singing and dancing and they called it prayer or they called it praise. And they said to the people who had been created like everything else from longing, remember that you are only water and wind but in this you are all things, for you are all time and space, even in your forgetting, and you must worship us, praising the water and the wind, by singing and dancing. When you sing and dance, when you are praising, you will hear the great hum of the universe and you will not be forgetting. And the people lived that way singing and dancing about the great light and the great darkness, and there was nothing but singing and dancing, and for those who could see, there was nothing, only the great hum and it was the universe still.

And the people lived that way in praise, from the beginning, but not all of them forever, not all of them and not forever.

"In The Beginning There Was Humming" is an excerpt from a novel-in-progress entitled *What Dinah Thought*.

Baby Town

BECKY BIRTHA

*M*imi sat very still on the high seat of the old Hudson. When her Aunt Berenice started up the car, it made a sound like it was trying to say its own name, but couldn't pronounce the "s." "Hudn, hudnnn, *Hud*nnnnn," as the motor finally got going. Now it was Aunt Berenice's car, but before that it was Granddaddy's. It was funny that his car was still alive, when he had been dead for a long time now. She wondered if Granddaddy, up in heaven or wherever he was, knew that she and her mother and sister were here in Virginia, visiting with Grandma and Aunt Berenice. She wondered if he knew that they were going for a ride in his car this afternoon, and if he minded. Did he know they were on their way out to his cemetary?

Anyway, he must like it that Aunt Berenice took such good care of his car, keeping the outside polished, and the inside always swept and brushed perfectly clean.

Against the back of her legs, Mimi could feel the soft rub of the gray-brown plush. The seats in Granddaddy's car were so deep that if she sat all the way back it made her legs stick straight out before her, as if she were a much younger child. She could see the toes of her Sunday shoes, their patent leather greased with vaseline, so that they gleamed even in the dull interior of the car. They were the perfect shoes—simple and unadorned, with plain round toes and a single strap — perfect little girl shoes, like the kind Alice in Wonderland, or any other little girl in a book might have worn.

This morning, all morning, she had felt, magically, as if she really were a little girl in a book. They didn't let her wear her hair out, yet, but this morning her grandmother had combed it into soft, twisted plaits that were much thicker than the way her mother made them. She had looked in the big oval hall mirror afterward and felt a touch of excitement. Usually looking in a mirror was a kind of disappointing surprise. She never looked the way she felt inside, like somebody special and not at all ordinary. But this morning, the part slanted off to one side, the hair lay flat and shining pulled back from her face, and the big, puffy braids hung almost to her shoulders. She looked like someone else. Like somebody that something magical and special might happen to at any time, maybe even this afternoon.

If she shifted a bit on the car seat, there was the comforting crumple of crinoline, her best slip, the one with the lace around the edges, and the double-tiered petticoats. And she loved the white dress, with its yards and yards of sheer fabric gathered into the skirt, and the delicate pink flowers embroidered along the edge of the yoke. It was much prettier, she thought, than Mindy's dress, which was longer and more grown-up looking, but not nearly so full.

She glanced at her sister, Mindy, who sat at the other end of the seat, separated from her by the old-fashioned arm rest that pulled down out of the seat back to make a big bulgy cushion between them. Mindy was watching out the window, lost in her own thoughts, her long legs doubled up beneath her with no particular regard for the wrinkles that that would make in her dress. Mimi faced forward again and leaned back, carefully, not to dislodge her hat.

In the front, the grown people were talking to each other, grown-up talk. "A whole lot's changed since you and Lewis left." Aunt Berenice was talking to Mommy. "This whole section —" she gestured out the open window, then returned her gloved hand to the wheel, "this whole section, Violet, from here to the city limits. And almost all of them have been sold."

"And it's the nicer class of people moving in, too," Grandma Devereaux put it.

Without even paying attention, Mimi knew who they were talking about—what they always talked about: colored people ... and white people. She concentrated on the houses they were passing, with their triangle roofs and big square picture windows. In front of one, a lady who looked like Aunt Berenice was holding a very chubby little boy by the arm, and locking the front door.

"Nice *respectable* people," Grandma was emphasizing. "Family people."

"You remember Jim Parsons, from Hampton? He and Ella just bought a lovely little place. It looks just like a picture postcard...."

From her place on the back seat, all Mimi could see were the backs of the three women's heads. But those were so different from each other, she might as well have been looking at their faces. All three of them wore their Sunday hats. Aunt Berenice's had a huge wide brim, with bunches of little apples and bananas around the crown. She must have picked it out on purpose to look as different from Grandma Devereaux as she possibly could. Grandma's hat was small brimmed, plain, black, and looked very severe and proper, pinned firmly with two fierce pearl hatpins to the coiled gray braids that wound around her head. Mommy's small blue hat, fitted close to her head, the faded bunch of lilacs on its side, bobbed between the other two, dodging every now and then to keep clear of Aunt Berenice's flaring brim.

Mimi put her hands up to touch her own hat, a white straw one with two ribbons tailing down the back. It looked a little bit like the hats that the girls wore in *The Five Children*. Everything about her was perfect today, she decided. Except maybe her knees.

She examined them now. There were still scars on them that were years old. There was a rough, round one that came from

41

the time Mindy pulled the wagon around the corner too fast, when Mimi was three. Was it ever going to go away? At least her legs were smooth and shiny, set off against the dust colored seat. There wasn't a trace of ashiness left on them. But they were a very dark brown. Much darker than Mindy's — maybe darker than her mother's. She felt a slipping, sinking feeling. Maybe it wasn't any use, to be all dressed up....

Still, Deacon Carter had said this morning after church that she was pretty. Well, he had been talking about Mindy, too, but that was all right. He had said to Aunt Berenice, "Miss Devereaux, who are these pretty little ladies we have visiting with us this morning?" As if he didn't know. He had made a show of taking his glasses off and putting them back on again. "So these are Mrs. Devereaux's granddaughters. Aren't they lovely?" And he had taken and shook her white-gloved hand, and then Mindy's, while his voice seemed to boom out over the whole church. "They're turning into real young ladies, aren't they? And how old are the young ladies now?"

Aunt Berenice had nodded to let her and Mindy know that even though it didn't sound like he was talking to them, they were supposed to answer. "I'm nine," Mimi said.

"And I'm eleven."

"Nine and eleven!" Deacon Carter drew it out, with his voice full of awe, as if nobody had ever managed to get to be such ages before. "Nine and eleven." And then, to Aunt Berenice, "It's a shame Mr. Devereaux couldn't be here with us this morning. I'm sure he would have been pleased."

Sometimes Deacon Carter came into Grandma's shop. He was likely to ask a whole host of Sunday school questions, while he waited for his clean shirts or his freshly pressed suit. Because she and her sister had Bible names, they always got asked about their namesakes. Did Mimi know who Miriam had been, in the Bible? What chapter was it in? Could she recite any of the verses? Mindy's first name was Martha, so Mindy always got asked all about who Martha was.

She remembered last summer, when Deacon Carter had come into the shop. Mimi had been all prepared and confident, the verses in her mind. Exodus Chapter Two, Verse Four. "And his sister stood afar off, to wit what would be done with him."

But this time Deacon Carter had folded his arms across his chest and said, "Well now, little lady, I want to know if you can answer me this. I want to know if you can tell me what the word 'integration' means."

He unfolded his arms and clasped his hands behind his back as he looked down on her. His gold watch chain and the gold that framed his glasses glinted and flashed at her. His tufted eyebrows looked like two question marks. How quiet it had suddenly become in the shop. The constant, choppy-choppy sound of the treadle of Grandma's sewing machine had ceased, in the corner. The big old press that her Aunt Berenice operated seemed to have stopped its hissing and spewing, seemed to be holding its breath. She could feel them all watching her, watching and waiting, like Deacon Carter. She had to think fast, trying to stretch what she knew into the kind of definition that teachers were usually happy with.

His big, deep voice spoke again. "In-te-gra-tion," he enunciated slowly, just like a teacher giving a spelling test. "You're big enough to know what that means."

"It means ... it's when ... when you take two different kind of ... things ... and ... and you mix them all up together."

He stared at her, through the thick square glasses. Then he pronounced, "It's when you take little white children, and little colored children, and send them all to the same school together. *That's* what integration is."

She had flamed with embarrassment. He kept on looking at her as if to say, "Now. What do you think of that?"

He thought she didn't know, but she probably knew more about it than he did! He thought he was so brilliant, standing up there over her like he was the superintendent of schools himself. Well, *she* lived in Philadelphia, where colored and white were just words — that was all — just words to describe the color of somebody's skin.

Finally Aunt Berenice came bustling up with the brown

43

paper cleaner's bag that held Deacon Carter's shirts hoisted on the end of her pole like a Sunday school banner. She laid it crackling across the counter, and Deacon Carter pulled out his wallet and forgot all about Mimi. She had been free to escape behind the counter, bruised and angry, yet still feeling horribly embarrassed, as if she had done something wrong.

That was a year ago, and she still felt embarrassed. Why couldn't she forget things like that? What did she have to go and remember it today for, today when all she wanted was to feel pretty, just like ... *any* little girl.

•

Now the car was pulling in through the gates, under an elaborate arch that read, "Restland Park." The talk in the front seat had changed. "I never did believe it." Aunt Berenice was shaking her head, the big brim of her hat swiveling back and forth. "Papa wasn't *that* sick. If he'd been able to get the kind of care he needed, he'd still be alive today."

"Now just stop, Berenice." Grandma Devereaux sounded exactly like a mother—nobody else could talk to Aunt Berenice that way. Mimi remembered that she *was* Aunt Berenice's mother, as well as Mommy's mother. "Those white doctors don't know a bit more than our Doctor Peterson...."

There it was again. No matter what they started out talking about, they always ended up on the same thing. She was never going to be like that when she grew up.

"I know, Mama, I didn't say that. It's the quality of the hospital I'm talking about. All that old, antiquated equipment. Junk so obsolete Riverside Hospital didn't have any use for it anymore—but the county figures it's good enough for us. And the facilities! You saw the room they had him in, with those uncovered pipes going right up the wall over his bed, dripping all the time...."

Mimi could scarcely remember her grandfather's death. There had been hurried packing, and the long drive at night. Then the familiar house, crowded with strange uncles and aunts she had never met, but who all somehow knew who *she* was. The aunts all seemed to be fat, and to be wearing dark shiny dresses. They'd crushed her against their stiff, slippery fronts and asked, "You don't remember me, do you?" Everything had been all mixed up, with Aunt Berenice sleeping downstairs on the sofa, and the lady from next door cooking in Grandma's kitchen. She and Mindy had not been allowed to attend the funeral.

Now Aunt Berenice parked the Hudson, and the five of them started slowly along the winding gravel road in the hot sun. The grass on either side of the road was parched brown. All over it were scattered the rectangular blocks of stone, some sharp edged and shining, others so worn they could scarcely be read. Mimi walked side by side with her sister, a little ahead of the grown-ups. She tried to imagine, or remember, what her grandfather's stone was like.

"See that big marble pillar, Violet, with the angel balancing on one foot?" Aunt Berenice's strong voice carried clearly across the short distance between them. "That's what Geraldine Lacey put up for her mother."

"Geraldine Lacey chose that?" Mommy's voice was surprised. "I never would have expected her to pick out anything so...."

"Garish," Aunt Berenice suggested.

"Well, yes, I guess. And she was always so ... thrifty, too."

"Thrifty!" Grandma Devereaux rolled the "Thr" and made the "ty" a sharp little tack. "Thrifty! Downright stingy is what I'd call it. If that girl really wanted to do right by her mother, she might have started sooner. It would have meant a good deal more to Myrtle Lacey if Geraldine'd spent some of that money on her when she was alive. How could a body rest in peace, anyway, with all that marble hanging there right over your head?"

Mimi caught Mindy's eye, and they both walked a little faster to get far enough away so that no one would notice the giggles. It seemed like you ought to be serious in a cemetery. You ought to be feeling sad and thinking about the people that had died.

"Do you think," Mindy asked after a little while, "that the dead people can see us, and they're all watching us?"

Mimi couldn't help looking around. But there was no one in sight — just the three grown-ups, far behind them now, and farther behind, other cars pulling in at the gate.

"I mean, what do you think *happens* to you after you die? Do you think you can still *know* things?"

"I don't know." She tried to think about how it might be. "Maybe it's nice. Maybe you can fly, and be invisible, and it's kind of like magic." When she was a very little girl, after Granddaddy Devereaux had died, Grandma had told her that now he was an angel up in heaven and he was watching over her. But she wasn't sure if even Grandma believed that. She couldn't picture Granddaddy doing anything as undignified as flapping a pair of wings. And she'd never seen him in his nightgown — he always had at least a bathrobe on. But still, she wasn't sure that he *couldn't* see her, in a different sort of way.

"Maybe they *can* see us. Maybe they're around us all the time, just kind of watching everything, like a play." It must be hard to do that, and never be able to join in, never be able to say anything. There must be things that they wished they could tell you. "Maybe," she said suddenly, intrigued with the new idea, "maybe when you're thinking about somebody that's dead, it's really *them* thinking about *you.*"

"But what if there's nothing," Mindy said, a devilish spark in her eyes. "What if you stop breathing and that's it. The End. Finished. Point Blank. Nothing."

She didn't believe it. It couldn't be like that. It was too scary to think about, and in her head she quickly chanted over the words to the bible verse "... that whosoever believeth in Him should not perish...." She wanted to talk about something else.

She said quickly, "How many different names can you think of for cemetery?"

"Graveyard," Mindy said promptly.

"Park."

"Park! That doesn't count."

"It does, too. The sign when we came in said Restland Park."

"Okay," Mindy conceded. "Um ... burying ground."

She had to think hard, and then she remembered. "Church-yard."

"That's only when it's beside a church."

"Well, a lot of times they are."

"This one isn't."

She looked around her, searching for more ideas. Now they were passing something that looked like a little house, built into the side of a slight hill. With a peaked roof and snug double doors, it looked almost cozy. A railing surrounded it, and a bit of hedge.

"Mindy!" She nudged her sister's arm. "Remember when we used to think cemeteries were Baby Towns?"

"Hey, yeah. I'd forgotten all about that. We *did* use to call them that. I wonder why."

"Don't you remember? We'd always be passing by in the car, and it looked like they were little cities and the gravestones were little houses. And we thought only babies must live there, and that was why everything was so small. I remember I used to think that was why they always had a fence around them, too, so the babies would be safe."

She could still picture the babies living here, quite free and happy, all by themselves without anybody to tell them what to do. She could picture them running about in diapers or little white nightgowns, perching on the headstones, or curling up to sleep in the shade under a rose bush, with their thumbs in their mouths. And at night, little flocks of them would disappear into those snug little houses. It would be like Never-Never land, and she could visit, like Wendy Darling.

The babies would run away laughing if anyone tried to catch one. But Mimi would be able to. It wouldn't be easy. She would sit for hours outside the little house where it lived. She'd keep very still and sing soft lullabyes. It would hear them from where it hid and, after a while, it wouldn't be frightened any more. She'd bring it toys and surprises, and leave them for it, right there under that crepe myrtle. Sunday after Sunday, she would come back, until it knew that she loved it, and it would

47

let her take it home.

"Mindy! Mimi! Girls! Right over here." The grown-ups had stopped, and crossed the brittle brown grass to one of the plots.

The gravestone was not remarkable. It was simple, plain but dignified, a little on the large side. Sure enough, her grandfather's whole name was carved neatly into the smooth flecked granite: Samuel Curtis Devereaux. The whole thing seemed so solid and permanent, so frank and matter-of-fact in the sunny daylight, it made her feel safe. Here was where her grandfather was buried. Here was his gravestone with his name on it. Here it would always be.

She tried to remember Granddaddy Devereaux. When he was alive, he had always made her feel safe, too. She had watched him at the shop, clamping the big press shut with his long arms, while it steamed and hissed, pumping its big flat pedal with his foot. He was the one who lifted the clothes down from the wires with the long wooden pole, and did all the things that Aunt Berenice did now.

In the house, at night, when she'd still been afraid of the shadowy stairway, and the gaping dark hall that waited between the top of the stairs and the bathroom, she could remember Granddaddy Devereaux going up the stairs with her, hand in hand. And when they'd got to the top, he'd lifted her up so that she could pull the string on the light herself. She wished she could remember more.

In the bathroom, over the sink, Granddaddy's shaving mug and brush and razor sat on the glass shelf, right where he'd left them. She knew his things, now, better than she had known her Grandfather. Once she had sat in his chair upstairs in Grandma's bedroom, when nobody was about, and tried to imagine what it felt like to be him. There was a hollow indentation in the smooth leather of the seat. And the chair itself had the odd, somber smell of old leather and dust, old rooms shut up and seldom used, old books — that always seemed to Mimi to be her grandfather's smell. But that had been only last summer, and long after he died....

"I wish he could have seen the girls now," Aunt Berenice

said. "He would have been so proud of them."

Would he? Mimi wondered. Proud of what? Would he have been proud of them for looking pretty? Somehow, she didn't think so. For having grown up so much? But everybody grew. It was something you couldn't help, and so couldn't really take any credit for. Maybe he would have been proud that they had gone to church this morning....

"Can me and Mimi—May Mimi and I go and explore for a little while?" Mindy turned from Mommy to Aunt Berenice to Grandma. You were never sure, when you were here, which was the right one to ask.

"Explore!" Grandma blew it out in a sharp little puff.

But Aunt Berenice said, "You mean just walk around for a little bit, by yourselves? I don't see any reason why not."

Now everybody turned to Mommy, and Mimi watched her glance from Aunt Berenice to Grandma before she came back to Mindy. "You know to keep on the paths, don't you? And keep your voices down...."

Mindy was already off, her long legs striding in big loping steps. Mimi had to skip a little, to catch up. She caught a whiff of that excitement returning, what she had felt this morning looking in the hall mirror, and again in the car, that feeling that something different and special might still happen to her today. And that she was ready for it, special enough to meet it. The skirt of the white dress flounced around her with each skip, and the hat ribbons bounced and tickled the back of her neck.

•

On the other side of the gravel road, across a little ditch, was a section where the grass seemed even sparser, even drier than everywhere else. It was mostly just patches of dirty sand. The headstones were much smaller and there was no sign of elaborate birds and crosses. The shrubbery and flowers that had set off some of the other plots were missing here, too. What was even stranger was that the plots seemed to be shrinking in size. Some were scarcely a yard long.

Mindy stepped right in front of the headstone of one of these shrunken plots, and read the inscription out loud. "Sandra Ann Waters. 1953 to 1957. Nineteen fifty-seven!" she repeated with surprise. "That was only last year!"

Mimi subtracted in her head. 1953 from 1957 left.... How could that be? Four years? "She was only a little girl." But how *could* that be?

And Mindy said exactly what Mimi was thinking. "How do you suppose she died?" They looked at each other, the wonder of it drawing them in close, and deepening.

Mimi turned back to the lettering in the stone. Sandra Ann. "They must have called her Sandy."

"Maybe she had pneumonia," Mindy said. "I know. Maybe she had leukemia."

It was so strange to think of a dead person being a little girl. There must be plenty of people who had known her, who were still alive. All her playmates. And maybe she'd had a sister. Would her sister have been allowed to go to the funeral? Did she get to have all of Sandy's toys and dolls, afterward? If anything every happened to Mindy, Mimi would take good care of her dolls. And her Sunday dresses, when she grew into them. What had Sandy's parents done with *her* dresses? "I wonder what she looked like," she said aloud.

"Well, she must have been colored, because Grandma said this is a Negro cemetery."

"So what?" Mimi flared. What did Mindy have to say that for? She sounded just like a grown-up.

Mimi plunged past her and on to the next plot, loudly reading the inscription on its stone. "Linda Christine Washington. Suffer little children to come unto me: for such is the kingdom of heaven." She went on to another. "Otis Mobley. 1945." And now she came to a plot where there was a freshly heaped mound of earth — but such a *little* mound! She stopped suddenly, the understanding finally coming to her. They were all children — that was what was wrong. This next one, right before her.... She stepped closer to read it, and then backed away. "Baby Girl Johnson," it said. "1958." Baby girl — she had not even lived enough of a life to be given a name!

They were spread out all over both sides of the path, more and more of the little plots. All those children—more than all the kids on her block back home—all those children—dead.

She spun around and took another narrow path, one that seemed to be headed back. She walked quickly; she didn't want to read any more. But the words seemed to flash out at her as she hurried by. "Beloved daughter of Charles and Mary Danby." "Beloved Son." "William Nathaniel Bishop. 1949 to 1951." In spite of herself, she stopped. Nineteen forty-nine. Her stomach plunged. Nineteen forty-nine was the year she had been born.

She glanced around, hoping she would find Mindy beside her again. But Mindy was crouching over another stone several yards away, her back turned to Mimi and the hem of her white dress hanging in the dust. Away across the road, Mommy and Grandma and Aunt Berenice were still standing there back where she had left them. Grandma had put up that black umbrella she always carried for a sunshade. Aunt Berenice was fanning herself with her hat. The three of them looked small against the great, bright sky. Nobody was looking her way.

Without her being able to help it, her eyes slipped back to the carving on the stone. Nineteen forty-nine. It could have been her.

She whirled about and fled down the path. But it wasn't leading the way she'd come from. All of the paths, now, seemed to veer off at crazy angles and run wherever they pleased. And the graves weren't laid out in neat orderly rows any more but seemed to go every which way—end to end or crosswise—jammed together in no pattern at all. She had to pay close attention not to step in the wrong place by mistake.

She felt surrounded—as if all that crowd of children were there, silently watching her. And then, abruptly, the path drew up short and ended.

The last two small graves were side by side against a rusty wire fence. Above one was erected a simple wooden cross—two sticks of wood nailed together and sunk in the sandy ground. Above the other was a thin plank, also wood, cut with a rounded top to imitate a headstone. Both of these markers had been painted white, and on both the paint was worn away, so that only faint traces still clung to the dull ashy brown of the wood. The two little graves lay side by side, as if the babies they sheltered might have been kin — they might have been sisters. If they had had names, no one would ever know what they were.

She couldn't stop staring at the bare wooden cross, at the plank that already leaned lopsidedly forward. It wasn't fair! It wasn't fair that this was all there could be for these two babies. All there would ever be for the rest of eternity. Old worn out sticks of wood stuck off in a corner by a rusty wire fence. No rose bushes or surprises or lullabyes, no snug little houses in a town all their own, nothing else pretty ever again. And it wasn't just because they were poor, either — she knew it wasn't only that. There was something else. The real reason was that they were colored. And this was what poor colored babies got. In the end, it *did* matter, after all. Everybody got sorted out, and here was what you got. This was how they treated you. It was mean and cheap and shabby and it was not fair.

She stood over the improvised markers for a long time. She wanted to run away, but she couldn't move. Her hands clutched at the black plastic strap of the Sunday pocketbook. Inside the white gloves, her fingers were moist and sticky, the fabric damp between them. The sun beat down on the crown of her hat, and the thick braids hung like fur on the back of her neck. She could feel the droplets of sweat running at her temples and standing out on her upper lip, feel the sweat sticking her underclothes to her body, under the too-tight bodice of the stiff white dress.

•

She pulled way over into the corner on her side of the seat on the ride back, and shut her eyes. She could still feel the tears all plugged up in a salty lump that strained against her throat, feel them stinging the backs of her eyelids.

She wouldn't let anybody make her go for a Sunday drive,

ever again. If they tried to tell her she would have a good time, it would be a lie. If they said they were going to a nice, pretty place, that would be a lie, too. Next time, they would just have to let her stay home.

She didn't want to see anything out the window, and she didn't want to hear anything anybody said. But Grandma Devereaux was talking. "Go on around the block, Berenice," she said. "Go past the new school. I want Violet to see where the girls would be going to school, in case she should ever decide to come back here to live."

"Are we maybe going to come back and *live* here?" Mindy asked.

Mimi opened her eyes. Mommy was shaking her head, saying quickly, "Oh, no."

"That school's going to be integrated, you know," Grandma said to Mommy.

Why couldn't they stop all that talk? Why couldn't they ever just hush?

"And the school board's just as provoked as they can be. They thought they were getting off the hook by building us a new school." Aunt Berenice chuckled. "You can bet if they had known they would have to integrate, they would have saved themselves the trouble."

Mimi had a sudden urge to throw back her head, open her mouth wide and yell and yell and yell. Make all the noise she could and cover up everything they said. Fill in every little crack with noise, so that the whole car would be just a solid block of loudness, blaring down the road. She would be loud and bad and rude and just let her voice stream out on and on so that nobody could say anything else, ever again.

She shut her eyes again, squeezing them tight. She bent her head down, and put her thumbs up under the fat braids and held her ears shut. The voices, the car motor were gone. But there was still another sound left, thrumming loud in her stopped up ears. It was the sound of her own blood, roaring like the ocean.

Downstairs, they were setting the table for dinner. She could smell the yeasty rolls browning, and the smell of the ham hock cooking in with the fresh greens. The aroma wafted up to her through the grating in the floor that Grandma had told her was there for the heat to rise through and warm the upstairs in the wintertime. If you looked down through the grating, and were quiet about it, you could see everything that was going on in the dining room, without anybody knowing you were watching them. But Mimi did not get up to look now.

She could hear, anyway, what was going on. She could hear the silver, the heavy pieces of flatware that had been in the family since the Spanish American War, clanking together as the drawer under the table was pulled out. And then the clink of the thick, ornate china plates being taken from the glass-doored cupboard. She could hear Mindy laying them, one by one, with a muted thud, on the cloth covered table. She could hear all their voices, Mindy's voice rising above everything.

"Isn't there a law about it, that says people have to be buried in a cemetery when they die?"

Somebody answered in a low voice, Mommy or Aunt Berenice.

"But doesn't it cost money to buy a ... don't you have to pay to get somebody in?"

A surprised laugh. More low answers, explanations, corrections.

And then, "Well, what happens if somebody dies and the person's family doesn't have any money — but the person is already dead?"

She couldn't hear the answers. She was glad she couldn't hear. She already knew what they were, anyway. In her mind, there was still the stark image of those two little graves, side by side under the bald wood of their makeshift markers, out there beside the rusty wire fence. She would never, never forget it. It was almost as if some part of her would always be out there too, unsheltered and exposed on the flat sandy ground, out under the open sky with them.

Downstairs, the grown-ups and Mindy were still talking.

She didn't listen. She drew her knees up and wrapped her arms around them, leaning far back in the Granddaddy chair. In another minute they would be calling her. She would have to go. But for a little bit longer she was safe and hidden, here between the angular arms of the old chair. She curled up even closer.

The familiar scent rose all around her—the scent of old leather and dust and something like ... shoe polish ... waxy and warm. It was such a long ago smell.... It was almost like having someone with her, holding her. Someone who had seen what she had seen, and who understood. She leaned her face against the back of the chair, pressing her cheek to the soft, worn, ancient leather that was smooth and brown and comforting, like skin.

Why The Sea Is Salty

KITTY TSUI

A long time ago when the ocean water tasted like rain, there lived in the mountains an old woman. She had long white hair streaked with gray that fell past her knees. Her skin shone with the oil she extracted from the needles of a rosemary bush that grew outside her cave.

One day a crane was flying in the heavens scanning the earth for food when it saw a silver mass shimmering in the water below. Thinking it was a school of fish, the crane began its descent. However, as it got closer the bird saw, not multitudes of fish, but a creature with a silver mane. Forgetting its hunger, the crane settled on an overhanging branch to watch this curious beast.

The woman laughed her welcome. She shook her head wildly, her hair flying in dancing sheets about her body. In her frenzy she began to sweat, releasing rosemary oil to the air. This pungent smell drew the crane closer and closer to the woman until it was standing in the water between her legs. With a motion of her head, the woman flung her hair over her body like a covering and pulled the bird gently against her.

The crane fell into a deep sleep cradled in her arms.

Some months later, on a night of the full moon, the stillness in the mountains was shattered by screams. Eagle, owl and raccoon stopped. Eagle tore open the night with her keen eyes.

56

She saw the old woman squatting at the mouth of the cave.
In the early hours of the day, a child was born.

Years passed. The child grew to maturity but she was unlike any child you and I have seen. From her kin, the crane, she had inherited a long neck and a covering of white feathers which ran down her neck and chest and ended just below her breasts. She had the blue-black hair of her mother's youth and strong, sturdy limbs.

Her mother taught her to live the way of the creatures. She ran the hills sure of foot and swift as the deer. She swam and played in the river surrounded by many minnows. She understood the language of the sparrow hawk and the cicada. She greeted the rising sun with a song and the setting sun, a dance.

For nourishment mother and daughter drank from the clear waters of the river; this was their food and water. They needed nothing else.

Crane girl had grown into a beautiful young woman. Her body was smooth and brown, the muscles rippling under the dark skin. The white feathers were a striking contrast to the rest of her.

Now the old woman had lived a long time. The years had etched deep crevices on her face and hung heavy on her limbs. She could no longer match the energy of her daughter. She was very tired and she wanted to rest.

One night young crane woman was awakened by loud thunder. Her mind was groggy. She blinked her eyes, coming out of a dream. She lay suspended in her own warmth on the bed of pine needles. Suddenly she realized that her mother was not sleeping next to her. She jumped out of bed and ran to the mouth of the cave. Outside rain fell in sheets. A sudden gust of wind soaked her. She was about to draw back into the warmth of the inner cave when she noticed a pile of silver hair at her feet. Stunned, she bent over and took a handful. She burst into a loud cry. Her mother's beautiful mane was laid out on the floor of the cave.

•

Meanwhile, high in the heavens in the Realm of Clouds dwelt the clan of Poa Poa Lung. They were makers of rain and riders of the rainbow. They lived in the clouds and were the guardians of the sacred lakes, the pure water that fell as rain onto the earth.

The dragons drank the water and roamed the heavens. The gods called them riders of the rainbow because of their ability to change the color of their bodies to the surrounding environments. That is why we cannot see a dragon flying in the sky. It was also said that when a dragon visited the earth she rode on the back of a rainbow.

Poa Poa Lung ruled the clan with a circle of elders. Some time ago her mate, Lung Goong, had sighted one of the first human women, fallen in love with her and taken her as his lover. Of course all the dragons had disapproved of this action. But by the time it was decided to banish them, the woman was heavy with child and could not travel. It was a long, painful labor. The woman was torn apart when her child was born. Lung Goong took her remains back to earth and was never seen again.

The offspring of this union remained, at the insistence of Poa Poa Lung, who was fascinated with the body of this creature.

Most people think of dragons as huge monsters but they are, in fact, small creatures only a head or two taller than the average human. They have a long, lizard-like body covered with scales and a short tail. Their heads are big, eyes bulging from the bridge of the nose; their jaws are prominent. Despite such a formidable appearance, they are very gentle creatures.

The child of the earth woman was as tall as a dragon but she had the body and hair of her mother. The only resemblance she bore to a dragon was in her hands and feet. In place of fingers and toes she had long root-like projections similar to claws.

They called the child Siew Lung and doted on her as if she were a dragon offspring. They adored her smooth body and envied her hair, small face and delicate neck. But the lines of her jaw, her shoulders and arms were sharp, strong, and the temperament of Lung Goong pulsed in her blood.

Each family looked after a lake. Since childhood Siew Lung had lived with different dragons but now she drifted about from place to place doing whatever she fancied. Unfortunately, she had gotten so vain that she spent most of her days admiring her reflection in the water.

Now the Realm of Clouds is vastly larger than any land mass you or I can imagine. It took much work to keep a check on the flow of water and to regulate the amount of rain that fell, so flooding would not occur.

All loved Siew Lung but there were those who were jealous of her beauty. It began as idle chat but the eviltalk grew and grew until it reached the ears of Poa Poa Lung.

"The Little Dragon is lazy and sets a bad example to all."

"She entices the young to play when there is work to do."

"She admires herself in the holy waters all day."

"She is plagued with an unnatural body. What if other dragons mated with humans?"

"What if her kind took over the Realm of Clouds?"

Poa Poa Lung had never been close to Siew Lung. But when she was called upon by the circle of elders to tell the young one of her fate, the old one shed tears.

"Siew Lung, you are banished from the Realm of Clouds until the day you rid yourself of vanity and laziness."

•

Meanwhile, below the heavens, many moons had passed since the old woman's disappearance. Crane woman talked with swallows and goats. But none had news of her mother. The storm that had awakened her on that fateful night raged on.

Crane woman lay in bed and cried. She missed her mother. She did not sleep and did not move from where she lay. Finally, she lost consciousness.

When crane woman came to, she was holding herself in her arms.

The storm had subsided. Flocks of birds sang and the mountainside awoke and rang with activity. Crane woman stepped gingerly out of the cave into the bright daylight. She dropped to her knees and put her lips to the soft, soggy earth. Then she went to the river and drank from the swollen stream. She climbed to the top of the mountain. The sight she saw made her cry out. A rainbow of colors stretched from horizon to horizon.

Everything around her oozed wetness. Her heart opened like a sea anemone. She breathed the sweet scent of the forest and for the first time in many moons, she was glad to be alive. Suddenly, above the excited chirping of the birds and the dripping of the forest, she heard unfamiliar noises. It sounded like a creature in distress, wheezing and out of breath. Crane woman did not waste any time but sprang off to investigate.

The noises led her past a clump of ancient redwoods. There, in the middle of a clearing, sat a strange-looking beast, sobbing and rubbing its eyes. Crane woman did not know if she was awake or in a dream because the beast was rather difficult to see. In fact, she looked right through it and saw the earth on which it sat. Swallowing her surprise, she asked, "Pray tell, gentle creature, what is the matter?"

Siew Lung jumped to her feet and shouted, "Who's there?"

Crane woman walked out of the trees and approached the beast, "I am daughter of crane and daughter of woman."

Unfortunately for the dragon, along with being banished, she could see neither herself nor anything that was close to her.

"I am lost and far from home. I am tired and hungry and I cannot see where you are."

"Are you without sight?" crane woman asked.

"Only if you are close to me. Step back to where those trees are and I will be able to see you."

Crane woman did as she was bidden.

"Oh my," exclaimed the dragon, "we look alike."

Though it was harder for crane woman, she could see what the other meant. They had the same face, the same limbs, the same body—save for crane woman's feathers—and both had long hair.

"I am called Siew Lung, Little Dragon. My father was Lung Goong and my mother was a woman."

Crane woman could hardly contain her astonishment. "Then

you are my kin! Welcome to the mountain. Let me take you to my home and you can rest and eat." She took Siew Lung by the arm and guided her to the cave.

"What do you eat in your land? Berries, leaves or grass? Or," she added, without hiding the disgust in her voice, "do you eat the bodies of dead animals?"

"Heavens no," exclaimed Siew Lung, "I eat and drink only the pure water that flows in the clouds."

Crane woman was much relieved. She went to the river and filled a hollow gourd with water.

They spent the next weeks telling each other about their lives. Crane woman took Siew Lung on long climbs up the mountain and introduced her to animals, birds and fish. At first they were suspicious of a creature they could barely see. But they all loved crane woman and began to trust this stranger who was her friend.

In addition to her inability to see things close to her, the dragon had been stripped of a number of other things. She could no longer fly and had lost the power of total invisibility. Sometimes one could see just the outline of her body and other times one could see it more solidly.

The two became fast friends. Crane woman laughed and danced as she had never done before. But she could not forget about her mother and resolved to find her.

One night she dreamt she was walking across an expanse of sand. The sun beat down on her. Her feet were swollen and sore but she kept on. In the distance she saw a geyser bursting from the sand. When she got closer, the water had changed into a burning bush. In the yellow flames she saw her mother's face melting.

Crane woman woke up screaming, tears running down her face. Siew Lung held her and rocked her as she told the nightmare.

"Something has happened to my mother," she sobbed, "I must find her, I must help her." She struggled to get up but dragon woman would not let her.

"Tomorrow, tomorrow before the sun is up we will go. Rest

now, sleep now, little crane."

Early the next day the two friends prepared to leave. Siew Lung filled gourds with water. Crane woman took her mother's hair and braided it tight into two braids, interweaving hair with dried sprigs of rosemary. When this was done she wrapped the braids around her belly. They began their journey.

The going was slow. Crane woman guided her friend with her voice and at other times they walked together, hand in hand. "Will I ever regain my sight," Siew Lung wondered. "I will never spend time looking at myself. Never, never, I swear." But the only answer was the high-pitched scream of a hawk and the wind in the trees.

"Woman friend, do you think I will ever see again?"

"Perhaps on our way we will find some cure, or the right prayer that will help it back."

They followed the river downstream until they had left the mountain far behind. All of a sudden, the river dipped and ran bubbling into a huge hole ringed with rocks. The friends drank their fill and took what they could with them.

Crane woman led Siew Lung across another mountain. Little Dragon's root-like feet dragged heavily on the ground, leaving snaking trenches in their wake. Crane woman stopped, her words coming in spurts.

"Do we not have a drop? I'm very thirsty and about to fall."

Siew Lung wiped the sweat from crane woman's face and whispered, "We finished the last days ago. Let us rest in the shade until the sun sleeps."

The two friends, weak and spent, nested in each other's arms.

By the light of the moon the two forged a path through thick forest. In the daytime they rested in places of shadow and tried to regain their strength. One day Siew Lung had blackouts.

"We must have water, we must have water," chanted the delirious little crane, leading them round and round in circles.

"I hear a river," shouted Siew Lung and they quickened their steps. But hours later they had not found it. Perhaps it had been the wind spirits laughing in the treetops.

"We must pray for guidance," whispered the little crane.

"I don't know how to. Besides, what good is that going to do?" grumbled Siew Lung.

Little crane dropped to her knees. "First we must humble ourselves before the earth. When our hearts are open we can ask the spirits for help."

Then the two friends slept. They were awakened by loud noises. It sounded as if a large creature was moving rocks and trees and hurling them from its path. A big black bear was smashing through the undergrowth. Crane woman pulled Siew Lung up hurriedly for they were right in its path. The bear did not see them until it had almost stepped on the Little Dragon's big toes. It looked from one to the other with startled eyes.

"What a strange pair! What are you doing here?" asked the bear in a gruff voice.

"Looking for my mother," whispered the weak crane, "and her vision," nodding at her friend.

"Your mother and your vision," laughed the bear. "Why I've never heard of anything so funny in all my years!" Great gusts of laughter shook the enormous belly of the bear.

"Yes, and we're lost and hungry ..."

"Hungry!" bellowed the bear, "hungry! Why, you're in the great forest surrounded by food." It hesitated, "What do you strange beasts eat? Not bear meat, I hope."

"Oh no, water."

"Water! Well, that's easy. Follow me, I'm on my way to the river for a midnight snack."

Much later the bear was asleep with a full belly, crane woman was floating in the water, and Siew Lung was sitting on a rock.

"How do we know if we're going the right way?" Siew Lung asked, "we don't even know where we're going."

"I have to trust my heart," replied crane woman blowing water out of her mouth.

"Chee!" shouted Siew Lung with disbelief, "why don't we ask the bear? Even in the clouds we know the bear is a wise creature. She'll help us. Bear, bear, are you sleeping?"

"Ssssh. Don't wake her. She is sleeping."

"But I want my sight back and I want to fly again. All this walking wears me out," whined Siew Lung. And with that she began to cry loudly, sneaking peeps at the slumbering bear.

"What's all this racket about?" growled the bear.

"I can't see," sobbed Siew Lung, "and my feet hurt. Can you help us?"

"You will learn, young one, that when you are punished, the way back is not easy. And," turning to crane woman, "as for your mother, I cannot say ..."

"Then you know about her!"

"All I can say is, find the Golden Rabbit and the truth will be known."

"How? Where?"

"I will say no more. I am grouchy and I hate being awakened when I am not ready to be. Now off with the both of you."

"But, bear, where?"

"Purity flourishes in open fields. Go. Grandmother moon watches over you."

With that the bear turned her back on them and went to sleep.

The friends continued, passing mountain and meadow. One day they stood at the edge of a bamboo grove looking over a sea of sand that stretched to the horizon.

"Little crane, are we going to cross the sand?" asked Siew Lung, staring wide-eyed at the desert.

Crane woman nodded.

"Yes, after a rest we will cross and be close to the end."

"We will? How do you know that?"

"I feel it."

To tell the truth, crane woman was feeling lost and discouraged. She did not know how much further they would have to go but she did not want Siew Lung to know her despair.

When the moon rose they started across the desert. Weeks passed. The sandscape had not changed. Their water supply was almost gone. Little crane was weak from lack of water.

"Siew Lung, take my mother's hair from around my belly

and go on. Leave me. I cannot go any further."

Little Dragon knelt beside her and started to cry. "I cannot leave you. You are my friend, the first I have loved besides myself." She put her face next to the little crane's and let her tears fall. Their tears spilled onto each other's dry, cracked lips. Despite her friend's protests, dragon woman carried her on her back and they continued on.

By the light of the moon they saw a huge shape towering in the distance. Siew Lung said, "It's a tree, a huge palm." Indeed it rose fifty feet into the night sky, its fronds an immense umbrella ringing the thick trunk. It grew, a luscious living jewel out of the barren land. They hastened toward it to sleep in its shade.

When the sun was high and the palm cast no shadow, the two friends were awakened by the fierce heat. They moved closer to the trunk, hoping for some relief. There was none. Suddenly, they were startled by a voice.

"Kind ones, spare me water. I have had none for many years."

"Who is it? Where are you?"

"I am palm. My fronds grow yellow at the tips. I need water."

"No," shouted Siew Lung, "we have only the last drops. Palm, you have lived years without water. We will die. We cannot give you any."

"Siew Lung, maybe we can spare some. How can we deny this palm? We have been resting in its shade. Without it we may have died sooner."

"No," repeated dragon woman.

"Please, I beg of you, let me have water. Though you do not see, I am dying a slow death. Please, I beg you, spare me water."

"No, no water."

Crane woman looked at her friend with sadness in her eyes.

"I will give the palm my share of the water."

"No," screamed Siew Lung. But it was too late. Crane woman had emptied the contents of her gourd into the sand.

Siew Lung sighed. "Then I will have to share mine with you."

"I do not want it. If you are true about sharing, give it to the palm."

"But ... but it is the last. There is no more."

"If you are true, give my share to the palm."

Siew Lung hesitated. Then in a swift motion, she too, emptied her gourd at the foot of the palm.

At that instant, they were thrown off balance by a strong gust of water that shot into the air. The palm had turned into a geyser. They were underneath a fountain of water.

They stayed under the geyser for many days. Siew Lung was content to play in the water but crane woman was anxious to move on. They had been following the stars in a northwesterly path. Crane woman was suddenly struck by a feeling that they were not going in the right direction. Try as she may, she could not shake the feeling.

"What is the way," she asked herself over and over. She told dragon woman of her uncertainty but Siew Lung had no ideas either.

One afternoon dragon woman pointed out a cloud to the little crane. "Up there. Does that not look like a face?"

Crane woman squinted. A cry burst from her lips.

"That is my mother!"

"Your mother?"

Sure enough, high in the sky was the old woman's head; the eyes were closed and the head was bald, like that of a newborn child.

Little crane strained her head upward. The face stayed with them for only a few moments. The wind made the face wispier and wispier until it dissolved. Tears were running down crane woman's face.

"Ma ma ... ma ma ..." She searched the sky through her tears but the face was nowhere to be seen. Then, in the west she saw colors — faint shades of lavender, yellow, orange.

"Look, do you see what I see?"

"Yes, a patch of colors."

The two friends looked at each other. What did it mean? Why the face in the clouds? The patch of colors?

"Maybe your mother is trying to guide you," offered Siew Lung, "telling you to follow the direction of the colors."

"Why does she not come to me? Why are her eyes shut? Ma ma I miss you so. Why did she leave me, why?"

"Your mother is with you. She's above us, in the sky."

"She's gone," sobbed crane woman, "gone."

Siew Lung pulled the little crane to her and hugged her. "Your mother is not gone from you. She is watching over you like a star and showing you the way."

"But I miss her."

Dragon woman held her and stroked her feathers.

"Let us rest now. The way ahead has been shown. Sleep, dear one."

The desert sloped gently upward. They battled the sand that sucked hungrily at their feet. At the end of the third night, Siew Lung said she could smell a large body of water not far off. Soon they both heard the sound of a mighty river. The air around them was electric with motion. All of a sudden the ground in front of them dropped. They were face to face with the ocean.

"The sea," breathed Siew Lung. "I have heard talk but never thought it was so big!"

The two were standing near the edge of a cliff. By the first light of day they could see white crests swelling and breaking. Some ways out from shore a huge white rock rose out of the sea. Through the ages the waves had sculptured the stone into the shape of a huge fist with two fingers to the sky. As the sun climbed from the sand behind them, its yellow rays painted the rock with a golden glow.

A truth dawned on the little crane.

"Siew Lung, we have found the Golden Rabbit!"

They were so excited they could hardly stand still. Unfastening the gourds from around them, they took off in opposite directions to look for a way down. The cliff dropped straight to the water. Its face was smooth and afforded not even the slightest toehold.

"How are we to get across?"

But the waves gave them no answer. They looked helplessly out to sea.

In the distance Siew Lung saw a flock of birds headed toward the cliff. As the birds got closer, they could see they were huge; the wingspan was triple the size of other birds.

"Albatross," said crane woman. "I have an idea. We will ask the birds to take us across. Albatross, will you help us?"

The birds hovered above them.

"What is it you wish?" One of them sang out.

"Please, could you take us to the white rock?"

"We are going to nest, we are going to nest," chorused the birds.

"Please, we must get across," shouted Siew Lung.

"Must!" mimicked one in an arrogant tone, "must, they say!"

"What will you give us in return?" screeched another.

"We have nothing but the gourds," shouted crane woman.

"What's in them? What's in them?"

"Water," replied Siew Lung.

"Water! Water! We live by water. We don't need water from you!"

Crane woman unwrapped one of the braids and held it up.

"I will give you my mother's hair. You can line your nests and your young will be warm."

"Ha ha ha, yes, yes ..." they screamed.

One of the birds swooped down and snatched up the braid in her bill.

"I will take you across. Grab my feet, one in each hand."

"What about my friend?"

"One braid for each of you," laughed the birds in unison.

"But, please, the other is all I have to remember my mother."

"One braid each, one braid each," sang the birds.

Siew Lung sank to the ground. "Little crane, go without me. Find your mother. Don't worry about me."

"You are my sister. We have come all this way together. You did not leave me. I will not leave you."

And with that she took the remaining braid and offered it to the birds.

The shore was left far behind. The smallest of the three albatross led the way; the other two carried crane woman and Siew Lung. Below them, the rock glistened like fine jade.

"We're here, we're here at last!" And the two jumped up and down and hugged each other till tears were welling in their eyes.

They walked around. They looked up at the giant fingers. They looked down at the waves. They looked at each other. Nothing grew on the rock; it was as smooth as an egg. They sat down. The rock was warm, heated by the sun.

"So we have found the Golden Rabbit. But it is not even alive! It is a rock! How is it going to help us?" shouted Siew Lung.

"I don't know ... I don't know ..."

The two friends sank into exhaustion and slept.

Crane woman entered the land of dreams. She was young crane girl playing in the river. She saw her mother coming toward her, arm outstretched. There were three small pebbles, in her palm. She gave them to her daughter. The old woman turned and looked at herself in the water. Without a word she walked deeper and deeper until the river swallowed her. Crane girl felt no alarm. She held the smooth stones in her hand and put the coolness to her lips.

When she awoke the moon was big behind wispy clouds. She thought about her dream and felt strangely exhilarated. She looked at her sleeping friend and felt a sudden tenderness toward her. A desire to touch Siew Lung's body overwhelmed her senses. She leaned and shyly planted a kiss on her cheek. Little Dragon stirred.

"Uuumm ... what is it?"

"I ... I think I love you."

They fell into each other's arms. Their kisses were at first awkward and shy. But it was as if their insides were on fire and the flames soon spread over their whole bodies. Their hands lingered over each other's back, thighs, faces. They kissed long and deep. Siew Lung nuzzled her face in crane woman's feathers. She took her nipple into her mouth and gently sucked on it. Crane woman felt delirious. Soft moans escaped from her lips. Siew Lung's mouth moved down to crane woman's belly. She stroked the place of soft feathers between crane woman's legs, parted them and kissed her. Crane woman thought she would faint. Every pore in her body cried out with joy.

Siew Lung felt light as a butterfly. She was soaring in the clouds, her body glistening, her hair flying about her. She heard her friend moaning her name and her heart danced madly as she answered back.

The two fell asleep locked in an embrace.

Siew Lung woke first. The sun was warm on her body. She felt crane woman against her and she smiled. She wanted to stretch but she did not want to disturb her friend. As she moved her fingers she felt something roll in the palm of her hand. She was holding three pebbles.

Crane woman stirred beside her. Siew Lung turned and saw her friend's beautiful face soft with sleep. She gasped. She blinked her eyes. The little dragon saw crane woman's face close to her for the first time. She could see!

She took in everything around her: the yellow light on the white rock; crane woman's hand on her stomach; her own root-like toes, solid as the rock. She wanted to shout, to sing. She wanted to share her joy with her friend. But she did not wake her. Instead she looked at the stones in her hand. How did they get there? She did not recall picking them up. Puzzled, Siew Lung looked at the ground around her. It was smooth; there were no loose stones.

Crane woman opened her eyes and looked at her friend with a shy smile.

"The corners of your mouth are so beautiful when you smile."

The little crane gasped. "Siew Lung, can you see?"

"Yes," she laughed. "Your eyes are a wonderful gray like the fog that covered us last night. Your skin is brown like the soil around your cave."

The two friends could not restrain themselves. They rolled around hugging each other and whooping with joy. Then Siew Lung remembered the pebbles in her hand.

"Dear friend, I have something for you. Close your eyes and open your hand."

As soon as she was given the stones, crane woman shouted: "It is three pebbles. They are white!" She opened her eyes and, indeed, they were.

Crane woman told her friend of her dream. They began to dance around.

"This white rock is a magical place," they sang.

"My mother came to me with three stones ..."

"And I woke up with them in my hand!"

A strong gust of wind hit them. Siew Lung stretched out her arms and leapt into the air. The wind carried her higher and higher on invisible wings.

"Little crane, I am flying, I am flying!"

Dragon woman soared above the white rock shouting with glee. Then she dipped her body and flew down to the crashing waves. The spray hit her face and wet her body.

Crane woman dropped to her knees and wept. She gave thanks for her dream and the gift of the white stones; she gave thanks for the return of Little Dragon's powers. For the first time she accepted that her mother was gone. But she had the white stones and she had a fine friend. And she had herself.

Crane woman climbed onto Siew Lung's back. They flew over the ocean, leaving the white rock far behind. After traveling for some time, Siew Lung sighted a beach and they stopped to rest. They lay on the warm sand. Crane woman had not spoken since they had left the rock.

"What is the matter?" asked her friend gently, "are you sad we did not find your mother?"

Crane woman shook her head. She got up and walked into the waves. She bent her long neck and looked at her reflection in the water. She saw something she had never seen before and gave a start. From the front of her head grew a thick streak of gray. She ran to her friend.

"Siew Lung, look!" She pointed at her hair.

"Oh, little crane, it is just like your mother's."

"Yes, yes ..." And she broke down in tears and laughter. "My mother is not gone. I am my mother! I am my mother!"

The two friends came together. They touched and kissed each other's bodies. Siew Lung nuzzled the salty tears from her lover's face. They breathed the fragrance of their armpits and explored the wetness between their legs.

In their ecstasy they rolled to the edge of the water. Siew Lung pushed her long fingers inside her friend. Crane woman gasped.

"Do I hurt you?"

"No, no, it feels good. Your fingers in me are roots. The fire in my heart for you is ancient."

"I love you," cried out the Little Dragon, "I have always loved you."

They made love by the edge of the water for a long time. Their orgasms exploded with the fury of tidal waves; their juices overflowed, mingling with the water.

That, my friends, is why the sea is salty.

"Why The Sea Is Salty" is part of a series of adventure stories about crane woman and dragon woman, illustrated by Ann Moriyasu.

Blood, Sweat, and Fears

DALE COLLEEN HAMILTON

*P*ain was her only reminder that she was not in a dream. Zia clutched her medicine pouch so tightly that her knuckles ached. Granny May had instructed her to bring along something special to the ceremony, and Zia had chosen to bring her hand-embroidered medicine pouch; a gift passed down from mother to daughter, to mark the occasion of Zia's passage from childhood to womanhood.

Zia's first bleeding lasted four days. On the fifth day, Kathleen contacted her closest women-friends, both from the reserve and from town, inviting them to attend a sweat ceremony in celebration of her daughter's womanhood.

Very few people from town ever come to the island. There's a sign at the ferry landing ... something about No Tresspassing on Indian Land ... that makes most white people feel unwelcome.

Even *fewer* people make the three-mile voyage to the south end of the island. The road is home to potholes and ruts and washouts, which deepen and widen themselves at the whim of the rain. It is more of a path than a road, and any vehicle attempting passage is brushed and slapped by overgrown Scotch Broom and Native Salmonberry bushes, both vying for earth and air and water and sunlight.

•

Kathleen rarely left the island, although she often went to the reserve to visit Granny May. Everybody on the island called her Granny May and everybody went to visit her from time to time. The kids would fill Granny May's kitchen and overflow onto the porch whenever word got out that she was gathering soapberries and planned to make a batch of "Indian Ice Cream." She'd whip the soapberries, adding just the right amount of sugar, until they turned into a bitter-sweet frothy treat.

And a lot of people went to Granny May when they were feeling sick. She'd brew them up a cup of tea made from herbs she'd gathered herself; sometimes pleasant-tasting, but usually bitter, made from gnarled roots and tubers dug high in the mountains.

Zia spent a lot of time on the reserve too, mostly at Emma's place. Both Zia and Emma had proclaimed each other as "best friend" and sat together every day on the ferry coming to and from school. A mysterious pattern had emerged: whenever Zia was feeling sick and couldn't go to school, so was Emma. And vice versa. This simultaneous sickness usually cropped up on sunny days. And both patients were often fully recovered by midmorning and begging to be allowed to play outside together.

Kathleen had to constantly remind her daughter about getting too much sun. Zia had the same red hair and fair skin as her mother and could never withstand the sun like Emma whose dark skin and Salish features seemed to absorb the sunlight and reflect it back through her eyes.

•

Zia relaxed her grip on the medicine pouch. She felt her mother's hand on her shoulder. She knew it was time. Followed by Granny May and the other women, Kathleen led Zia past the old mission chapel, through the orchard, and on to the sweat lodge at the edge of the creek.

Inside the sweat lodge, the air was laden with sweet smells. The fragrance of the freshcut cedar boughs cleared Zia's head.

She watched the women lay the boughs on the dirt floor of the lodge, creating a rich green mat around the central fire pit. Zia was handed an armful of cedar boughs. She followed the movements of the other women as they worked, awed by the amount of trouble they were going to for her.

When all the branches had been laid, Zia stood back and looked at the sweat lodge as if seeing it for the first time. Dogwood branches, bent into semi-circular arches, formed the framework of the lodge and were covered in layers of skins and canvas and blankets. The result was an igloo-shaped structure with a firepit in the center to hold the hot rocks. The lodge had a weather-beaten quality about it. Kathleen had built it before Zia was born, basing the design partially upon local Native tradition and partially upon her own ideas of how her Celtic ancestors' sweat houses must have looked. The lodge had become part of the landscape, like a huge gray boulder deposited by the ice age.

The rocks were being heated in a fire pit just outside the sweat lodge door. They'd been in the fire for most of the afternoon and were red hot. The fire was being tended by a very pregnant woman whom Zia recognized as Lyla, one of Granny May's many nieces.

The women began to take off their clothes. Some covered themselves with towels and robes, while others remained fully naked. Zia and Emma started with their shoes and socks but hesitated before taking off the rest. They were shy about exposing their bodies to the older women and waited until the last minute to tear off their shirts and pants.

Kathleen motioned for Zia to approach the door of the lodge, instructing her to move in a clockwise circle around the fire where the rocks lay ready. The other women fell into line, following Zia and her mother. The door of the lodge was low to the ground, necessitating that all those who enter crawl upon the earth.

It was dark and close inside, but Zia felt her mother's hand guiding her clockwise around the central pit, nearly full circle, to a position immediately adjacent to the door.

With the door still open, a dim light filtered into the lodge. Zia looked around at all the women who were getting themselves seated, as comfortably as possible, on the bed of cedar; some of them chattering back and forth, some stone silent. Then the entire circle fell silent. Kathleen asked Granny May, the oldest woman in the circle, to begin with a prayer. The old woman heaved a sigh and offered a prayer in her mother tongue. Zia didn't speak more than a few words of Salish, mostly swear words taught to her by kids on the reserve. But as she listened to Granny May, she found herself hanging onto every word. The sounds themselves, not the actual words, seemed to hold the meaning.

Then Granny May pulled an amber jar from her medicine pouch. One by one she touched each woman's lips with her finger, which she dipped from time to time into the ointment jar. Zia was at the far end of the circle and the last to receive the ointment. When Zia's lips were dabbed, she realized that it was not exactly ointment, but some sort of gooey resin. "Balsam pitch," whispered Granny May. "It helps the spirits find you and speak through your lips."

Zia took a deep breath through her mouth and the scent of balsam filled her head and seemed to spread throughout her body. With every breath, her head felt clearer and lighter and yet somehow detached from the rest of her body.

Granny May returned to her place in the circle of women and dabbed her own lips with balsam. Then she called out to Lyla, who appeared a moment later at the door of the sweat lodge. "We're ready for the rocks now, Lyla."

Lyla just nodded and disappeared. A thick silence fell as they awaited the firey rocks. Then Lyla reappeared, carrying the first rock, glowing deep orange, cradled in the antlers of a deer. As she passed through the doorway, she murmured a familiar phrase: "All my relations."

It was a phrase people often used when passing through the doorway of the sweat lodge. Granny May said it wasn't a local tradition; that an Indian man from the prairies had taught it to her.

Lyla knelt just inside the doorway. With the rest of the women naked, it looked strange to see her fully clothed. She lifted the rock, firmly clasped between the pair of antlers, to the edge of the central pit. Then she released the rock from the antlers and it tumbled into the fire pit; fire meeting earth.

As the rock passed Zia's leg on its way to the pit, she felt her flesh crawl. Only Kathleen knew of her daughter's nightmares: nightmares that sent Zia running to her mother's bed in the middle of the night; nightmares about fire. Kathleen watched her daughter's face as the next rock was hoisted into the pit. Zia's fear was written all over her face and in the way she re-coiled involuntarily as the rock came close to her leg. Kathleen knew this sweat would be a true test for her daughter.

Zia vowed not to show these women her fear. She closed her eyes as the next rock came near. This was not Zia's first time in the sweat lodge. She had sweated with her mother before, but as a child, not as a woman. In the past, she had not been al-lowed to come into the sweat lodge until the adults were fin-ished sweating and the rocks had cooled down, and even then she had sat on her mother's lap or at her side. She could barely see her mother on the other side of the circle where she seemed preoccupied in a silent prayer.

Lyla brought in several more rocks. Zia lost count of exactly how many. The air was becoming almost unbreathable, laden with particles of dust and soot from the rocks. Zia suppressed an urge to cough, not wanting to disturb the silence or to have anyone think of her as weak.

Then Kathleen called out to Lyla to close the flap on the door. Zia had never been in the lodge with the flap down. As a child, the door had always been left open to let in light and air. Zia held her breath as the darkness became complete. Her eyes searched the interior of the sweat lodge and found a tiny ray of light leaking in near the ground behind her. She fixed her eyes on that snatch of light, turning slightly from the circle to do so. But her mother spotted the light leak too and yelled out to Lyla to cover it up from outside. The only source of light was extin-guished. Zia turned to face the center again.

There was a slight glow coming from the fire pit. Zia squirmed to one side until her leg was touching the woman next to her. From that position, she could see into the pit. She inched her way forward until she could see the rocks more clearly. They were like huge molten eggs in a nest. The fire pit was the only source of light in the lodge, so Zia focused on it. Slowly, she began to feel her fear subside; not only her fear of the darkness, but also her fear of the fire.

A voice came through the darkness. It was Kathleen, and she offered a prayer. Zia saw the silhouette of a hand, and then an arm, rise up above the fire pit. Something was being dropped into the fire. Her mother's prayer explained, and she explained in such a way that it became a part of the prayer. Tiny pieces of sage and sweetgrass and cedar were being thrown onto the rocks. The herbs, upon contact with the intense heat, immediately ignited and sent up a waft of their perfume. Someone in the circle inhaled noisily and let out a sigh that seemed to ease the pain of labored breathing.

Granny May sang a song to the four directions. Another voice, which Zia couldn't recognize, called upon the ancestors to join them. As those words were spoken, a chill passed through Zia's body. She had the unnerving sensation that someone was standing behind her; that a whole line of people were standing behind her. Zia repeated the phrase she had heard earlier: "All my relations."

Another dark shadow appeared over the fire pit. Then the rocks came alive, as water met fire. They hissed and crackled and shot up clouds of steam. Someone had poured water over the rocks.

The lodge filled with hot steam, opening every pore in every body. Breathing that air was like breathing fire. It clung to Zia's throat and lungs. She held her breath until it seemed that her lungs would be torn apart. From somewhere in the darkness, she heard her mother's voice. "If it gets too hot for you, get down close to the ground. It's not quite so hot near the ground."

Zia crumbled onto the cedar bed, burying her mouth and nose into the branches. The heat was rising and Zia found some relief. Still, it was very near unbearable. Zia forced herself to think of the cool air coming off the ocean, the cool water in the stream just outside the lodge. Zia grabbed a handful of cedar from the floor of the lodge and held on tight, as if to anchor herself inside the lodge, to resist the temptation to crawl outside into the coolness and the light. She refused to leave. These women had come here to celebrate her womanhood. She refused to act like a child.

Granny May's voice cut into Zia's frantic thoughts. "... and if you have to get out, then get out. It's nothing to be ashamed of if you have to leave. This isn't a competition to see who can stand the most heat. If you can't stand it, just yell out, 'All my relations' and Lyla will open the door."

Beads of perspiration covered Zia's entire body and as those beads broke, they became streams of sweat which dripped off the end of her nose and trickled down her neck, her breasts, her legs. Only the thought of stumbling and falling into the fire pit kept Zia from making her way to the door.

Granny May's voice cut through Zia's pain and Zia drank up her words. The old woman suggested they each take turns offering a prayer or a song; or if they had nothing to say, to simply offer silence when it came to their turn. Granny began with a prayer in Salish. Zia raised her head from the cedar branches, just far enough to hear the music of the words.

Then it was Kathleen's turn. There was such a long silence that Zia wondered if her mother had nothing to say. But then her mother began, and offered a prayer in Gaelic, her own mother tongue. Kathleen had studied the ancient language for years and had taught Zia a few words and phrases. Zia raised her head into the scorching heat to hear her mother's prayer. Her head was swimming and she couldn't understand a word, but the rhythm of her mother's voice was comforting. On the last sentence, her mother switched to English: "May this child whom we are now welcoming as a woman walk with self respect and the respect of her ancestors."

Granny May let out a sound that anyone, speaking any language, could understand; several of the women echoed the sound: it was a chorus of agreement.

Kathleen continued. "Zia's own Celtic ancestors built sweat houses and used sweating rituals to cleanse themselves. May this woman-child of my own blood be cleansed of her fears. I call on the fire and the water and the earth and the air to cleanse this young woman."

Zia took a deep breath and rose onto her haunches. She rocked back and forth, allowing the waves of heat to hit her full force. Her dry lips parted and she let out a cry; not so much a cry of pain as a cry of sheer endurance.

More water was poured onto the rocks. The women in the circle continued to pray. Not everyone from town knew everyone from the reserve, so some introduced themselves before they took their turn to pray. There was Paivi, a Finnish woman who had been in Canada only a few years. She sang a song in Finnish, stopping and starting several times, either from the emotion or from the heat; Zia couldn't tell exactly what was making the woman's voice falter and stop and then grow strong again. Paivi translated the words of her song: it was a song about the Sauna traditions in Finland. Her voice broke again and even in the dark, Zia knew she was crying.

The next woman in the circle began. Zia recognized the voice as belonging to Dawn, her mother's best friend from town. Dawn was a midwife and delivered babies at home, whether the doctors liked it or not. She made medicines out of local plants, plants that most people call weeds. The song Dawn sang was one she'd made up herself. She sang it so quietly that Zia couldn't make out most of the words. But the chorus stayed with her:

> We have been here before
> And we'll be here again.
> The circle remains,
> Though we all wander far.
> So lift up your heart,
> You will never be alone.
> Let the earth be your medicine
> Forever.

There was only one more woman to speak, then it would be Emma's turn, and then Zia's. Zia began to panic. What could she possibly say that these women would be interested in hearing? She couldn't think of a single song.

The woman sitting next to Emma began. It was Carol, one of Granny May's daughters. She was a full-blood Indian, but she lived in town, just her and her kids, in an apartment building next to the new mall. She'd married a white guy and lost her Indian status. Now she had no status *and* no husband. In the sweat she prayed to get her status back, so she and her kids could move back onto the reserve. She didn't sing at all: she just said her prayer real quick and that was it.

Emma's turn. Zia was next. Emma sang a song that Zia had heard her sing before. It was a song that had been passed down through her mother's family. Emma's mother had taught it to her and told her to pass it on to her own kids.

Zia straightened her back as Emma sang. She tried to stop a feeling that seemed to come out of the darkness and hang over her head. She felt jealous of Emma and angry at her mother; angry because her mother had not provided her with a song to sing at her own womanhood celebration.

When Emma finished, there was a silence. Then Zia said the first thing that came into her head. She was as surprised as everyone else at the anger that came out through her words: "I don't have a song."

"You know lots of songs."

"Just stupid kid songs and Christmas carols. I mean a song like Emma's, a family song."

This time Kathleen responded. "We don't know much about our family, Zia. When they left Ireland, they left a lot behind. And when the church got strong, a lot of the old folksongs got forgotten. People stopped singing most of the old family songs and only sang when they went to church."

Zia needed to know more. "How can I find a family song?"

"All we can do is piece together what we can and create *new* songs."

"But I don't know how to make up a song."

Kathleen had no answer, so Granny May spoke her mind. "You have to listen, I mean really listen, to other people's songs. And then you have to pray for a song to come. Why don't you try praying for a song?"

"I don't know what to say when I pray."

"Sometimes the most powerful prayers are silent. Why don't we all pray together, silently, that Zia finds her song. Is that okay, Zia?"

"Okay."

•

In the silence that followed, Zia prayed for a song. But all she heard was the sound of the creek outside the lodge; and, at a great distance, a bird. Kathleen broke the silence by offering the women a drink. She passed around a wooden bowl which contained a special tea made from herbs in Kathleen's garden.

"The herbs in this tea are elder blossoms, mint and yarrow. They'll help to open up your pores so you'll *really* sweat." Then she called out to Lyla: "... ready for the next round of rocks."

Three more times the rocks were replaced with hotter rocks, and after each round, the steam rose hotter than before. Zia's only measurement of time was in the number of openings and closings of the door as Lyla came and went with the hotter rocks. After each round, Zia thought it must surely be the last.

On the third round, steam rose again from the rocks, huge clouds of it, entering every pore, every orifice, every fold of skin. As the steam rose, Zia's spine buckled and she crumbled to the floor of the lodge. The cedar branches beneath her felt like live coals. She leaped onto her haunches, searching the darkness for an escape route, like an animal caught in a forest fire. She knew that she had to get out, either through the door or by clawing her way through the layers of canvas behind her. She remembered what she had to do in order to leave the lodge. She whispered the words that would open the door, and then she screamed them, swallowing all pride: "All my relations!"

Lyla heard the muffled call and threw open the door. Zia lurched towards the light and fell into Lyla's arms. Lyla half-dragged, half-carried the steaming young body to the creek. Zia stumbled knee-high into the water. She reached down, her hands cupped, and scooped up a handful of cold creek water. She splashed it on her face, then down her back, her breasts, her stomach. She felt a shiver begin in her toes, working its way up her legs. But the coolness was shortlived: heat began to generate in her cheeks and spread like wild fire. So Zia bowed her head and dove under the water. She stayed under until her lungs seemed to force their way up her throat. Zia resurfaced and stood dripping in the middle of the creek. She rubbed herself. Pieces of dead skin detached themselves from her body and floated down the creek to the ocean.

Zia's head began to swim. The trees and rocks and everything around her took on a murky underwater quality. She felt her feet go out from under her. She was being carried down stream, carried away like a layer of dead skin.

Emma caught her under one arm, and Lyla under the other. They dragged her to the edge of the creek and sat her on a cool rock under a willow tree.

Zia tried to sit quietly, but shivers racked her body. And one recurring thought racked her mind: she had been the first one to leave the sweat lodge, the first one to give up. She had acted like a child. All the women were still inside the lodge. Zia closed her eyes. She felt someone's hand on her shoulder. Looking up, she saw Emma. Zia shook Emma's hand from her shoulder and closed her eyes again. For the first time in a long time, she wanted to be left alone.

Even with her eyes closed, the light, reflecting off the water, leaked into her field of vision. She kept them tightly closed, hoping the sound of the water would take her far away.

But there was another sound, a buzzing, which threatened to drown out the sound of the creek. The buzzing appeared to be inside her own head. She opened her eyes and shook her head, annoyed at the interruption. It was then she realized that the source of the buzzing was external.

A hummingbird was hovering a few inches away from her face. The hummingbird sang out. Zia attempted to imitate the song, hoping her crude sound would not frighten the bird away. For a second it was gone, in a flash of color; but then it was back, hovering even closer than before. It sang out again, but this time Zia didn't even attempt an imitation; she listened closely to the song. And between aerial acrobatics, the hummingbird repeated it over and over again. Then, without warning, the tiny bird lifted and was gone. Zia saw a tiny flutter of color floating towards her as the hummingbird departed. She shielded her eyes against the sun and reached out to catch it: it was a hummingbird feather and she caught it in her hand and held it, tight enough to contain it, but not so tight as to damage it.

She placed the feather carefully in the crevice of a rock. Then she edged her way to the creek and splashed her burning cheeks with cold water. Already the image of the hummingbird was beginning to fade, like a watercolor painting left out in the rain to bleed. Only the feather offered proof. Zia retrieved the feather from the rock and, cradling it in her hands, climbed the steep slope back up to the sweat lodge.

•

The door was closed. The women were still inside. Emma was sitting just outside the door of the lodge, wrapped in a towel. When Zia reached the door she sat down next to Emma. "They said we could come back in," whispered Emma.

Lyla appeared from behind the lodge and opened the door for them. A wave of heat hit Zia as she crouched to enter. Her nostrils flared at the smell of human sweat. Zia held the hummingbird feather even tighter. She and Emma crouched just inside the door, their eyes adjusting to the darkness.

Most of the women were lying on their backs or on their sides. They'd finished their last round. Lyla left the door open and the light fell across the women's naked and exhausted bodies.

Granny May spoke first, her words hanging in the steam-laden air. "How do you feel, Zia?"

"Okay. Ashamed." Zia was glad no one could see her cheeks.

"Ashamed? Why?"

"For leaving the sweat lodge before it was over."

"Why did you leave?" asked Granny May.

"Because I couldn't stand the heat any longer."

"That's no reason to be ashamed."

There was a round of agreement from the women in the circle.

"You're lucky to learn a lesson in humility now, Zia," added her mother.

Granny May nodded in agreement as she spoke. "Better than waitin' 'til you're so high on your horse that you'll really get hurt when you fall."

Zia, feeling their acceptance, relaxed the tension in her shoulders and jaw. She opened her hand and held out the feather for everyone to see. In response to their questions, Zia told the story of the hummingbird. The entire circle of women listened until Zia was finished with her story. Then they all wanted to see the feather, so it was passed around the circle. It was handed from person to person with great care. Some of the women were surprised that a hummingbird would come so close to a human being. Granny May didn't seem surprised. She said it was a sign, and then refused to say anything more about it.

There was a question Zia had been wanting to ask her mother, and feeling more confident now, she spoke it out loud. "Mom, how long could you stand it the first time you ever sweated?"

"Not as long as you. And I was much older. Sometimes it's harder to swallow your pride and get out than it is to stand the heat and pretend it's okay."

"Anything else you want to say, Zia?" asked Granny May.

"I'm still feelin' kinda sad that I don't have a song."

"It'll come to you. Sometimes it takes years. Songs come and go. A lot of our songs got lost when they sent our young kids away to residential school. In them schools, they wouldn't let the Indian kids sing their songs or speak their language. They taught them to speak only English and to pray to a God who musta been an Englishman, I guess. They dressed the Indian kids up in uniforms and gave them shiny instruments to play and taught them to be in marching bands. Those weren't our songs. We have our own songs."

"How do you know if it's your song?" Zia asked.

"You'll know your song when you hear it. Sometimes it comes from your ancestors. You should ask your mom more about your family. Do you know where your ancestors came from, Zia?"

"My mom's family came from Ireland and I don't know about my father's family."

"Your father's family was from Scotland." Kathleen's voice cracked, then became calm again. "But they came to Canada a long time ago, four or five generations ago. All your ancestors were Celtic, Zia."

Granny May seemed pleased. "Well then, maybe that's where you'll find your song. Or maybe you'll find it around here, since your family's been here a long time. Talk to your mom about it. Don't ever forget about your own ancestors."

Zia liked the way everyone was paying so much attention to her questions and would have gone on asking more, but Granny May leaned over to Kathleen and whispered something. Kathleen smiled and whispered something back.

Then Granny May spoke again. "You don't have a song yet, Zia ... but we won't have you leave this ceremony without a name. During your normal life, you'll still be known as Zia. But at special times, such as this, your name will be Swutzalee."

"What does that mean?" asked Zia, repeating the name to herself.

"Hummingbird."

•

The women nearest the door started to move out of the lodge, crawling on all fours in order to make it through the tiny opening. Zia knew it had been deliberately built this way to create a sense of rebirth. Now she was as reluctant to leave the sweat lodge as she had been to enter it.

Out in the cool early evening air, the women were taking turns dunking into the creek. The pool, which had been formed by damming up the water with rocks, was only big enough for one person at a time. As each woman entered the water, a noise would pass her lips; some voluntary, some involuntary. Some moaned quietly, some squealed, some let out howls that seemed to send the entire island into motion, like a boat anchored in a storm.

Zia looked up. Both the sun and the moon shared the sky. In the subtle light of early evening, Zia watched the women's naked bodies. She didn't want to stare, so she stole glances when she thought no one was watching. One woman had huge breasts which hung down past her waist, and rolls of fat that hid her pubic hair from sight. This same huge woman was being helped to her feet by a woman so thin and apparently frail that Zia wondered how she had ever withstood the heat inside the sweat lodge.

There were women with dark skin and with fair skin. There were women whose bodies some might deem worthy of admiration, and others whose bodies fashion magazines would not judge as "beautiful," furrowed and scarred from childbearing, hard work and time. But every body, regardless of color and build, reflected the same light from the moon and from the sun as they emerged, dripping wet, from the water.

Zia entered the creek last, and as she did, several women gathered around and took turns dumping buckets of cold water over her head. Every time the water hit Zia, she thought she wouldn't be able to stand another bucketful ... but every time she did.

Between buckets of water, Zia saw her mother gathering evergreen boughs. Kathleen approached Zia and began to scrub her daughter's shivering white body with those branches, moving from her outer extremities to her heart. Kathleen scrubbed until the skin was red. At first Zia found the sensation tingling and quite pleasant; but soon she was on the threshold of pain. She refused to cry out, and stood perfectly still while her mother scrubbed.

Then, to Zia's relief, her mother stopped and motioned for her to bathe again in the creek. Zia's body was covered in the essential oils of the branches used to scrub her. The full strength of those oils exploded in every pore as her limber body broke the water's surface. Zia immersed herself entirely in the icy water. It was easier this time. Then she climbed out of the pool and headed for the creek bank, where her mother was waiting with a towel held open.

Kathleen dried Zia's hair and wrapped her in the large towel. Then she walked to the creek's edge and threw the branches she'd used for the cleansing into the moving water ... and they were taken away toward the ocean.

The other women were already dressed. Granny May was looking like herself again, dressed in her usual cotton house dress, hockey jacket, and her favorite running shoes. If a casual observer were to see Granny May in the laundromat or the grocery store in town, they'd likely think she was just another wrinkly old Indian woman ... but Zia knew differently. Zia had sweated with Granny May and knew the power of her songs and her prayers. And Zia had witnessed other rituals performed by Granny May: funeral rituals, ancient rituals, rituals performed at the graveside when the church service was over and the priest had gone back to town.

Zia also had a new respect for her mother, whose songs and prayers in the sweat lodge had drawn Zia gently into the circle of women. Zia now knew that her mother could not simply give her a song. She would have to earn it.

Zia turned from the other women and looked up. In the distance she could hear a hummingbird sing.

Fruit Drink

BODE NOONAN

I went to church last Sunday during a hurricane. It was the first time I'd been since my father died. Has it really been so many years? I remember we sang the hymn "Jesus Savior, Pilot Me" especially for him and I had wanted to cry, but I wouldn't. Oh, don't think I went to church because of the hurricane. I've been through many storms before; and though some have made me think strongly about buying a boat and loading it up with a dove, an olive branch and two of everything I have in the house, this one seemed not so religious. Just a lot of rain that gave no indication of stopping and a wind that rendered umbrellas useless and raincoats only trappers of water.

I was feeling somewhat rundown — perhaps from all the swimming and biking and running I do to build up my physical strength — not to mention, a little hungover. So I drank some Knudsen's Natural Breakfast Juice, which I prayed would help heal me with, as it says on the label, its pineapple, white grape, orange, grapefruit, lemon, lime and tangerine juices from concentrates with natural citrus flavors. But I wasn't really sure that it contained all of those things and wasn't just tap water and sugar and questionable additives. I wasn't really sure I should be going to this church on the corner of Port and Burgundy Streets where I had been baptised in tiny white garments, and which has housed my family on my mother's side —

though my mom has splintered off to a church nearer her neighborhood now — literally for generations. But I had simply made up my mind. Neither my feeling under the weather, nor the weather itself, nor even the woman I love lying provocatively on the sofa asking me how on earth I could leave her on this cozy so good to be inside type of morning to go of all places to church would sway me from my quest.

I pulled my dress out of the closet, thought about pantyhose, pumps and a purse, and put it right back. I have a hard enough time recognizing God; I didn't want to make it hard for God to know me. I chose instead my favorite black I call them "Art Pants," black socks with little gray and white cats on them, my running shoes and a white heavy cotton sweater.

I wanted to run up the stone steps of my old church to the oaken double doors at the top, lifting my knees high and pushing hard off the balls of my feet. Yet I felt myself ascending one slow step at a time as if there were hands gripping the backs of my shoes. I felt small and frightened with the wind and the rain whipping around me under the darkening sky. I was afraid that the bells would start pealing, the building would begin to shudder, crack and crumble, and the steeple would topple, the cross at the peak of it plunging deep into my bosom. I imagined that Jesus His Very Self might step down from the huge mural I remembered encircling the altar where He stands with His pierced hands outstretched, surrounded by angels, humbled parishioners and sheep, His flaming forefinger pointed at me, His celestial voice thundering, "Unclean! Unclean!"

I stepped in. It was early. The church was quiet, almost empty. I shook off a storm that seemed impotent now that I was inside this strong, sturdy building. A man with white hair gave me a bulletin and smiled. I saw a cardboard box decorated with wrapping paper with a slot cut out in the top of it to collect donations for the victims of the earthquake in Mexico. The mural was much smaller than I had remembered. I walked down the aisle, picked a pew not too far to the front, not too far to the back, to the right and sat down. I felt like I wanted to cry, but I didn't.

I felt isolated and different from the arriving husband and wife couples, the sometimes pious sometimes scampering children, the elderly ladies in their matching hats and gloves. I suddenly wanted to jump up and run, a heathen escaping her captors, until I looked up and saw someone who looked just like me. It was my aunt—my mother's younger sister. She and I have almost exactly the same face.

My aunt never married, but she's lived with the same woman since college. She assures me that they are not gay. My aunt and her womanfriend are of different faiths, so my aunt worships alone today as do I. She doesn't see me, yet walks to the very pew in which I am sitting. She stands to pray for a moment, resting her age spotted hands on her umbrella as if it were a cane. My God, she's in her seventies now! She was in her seventies the last time I saw her, but somehow I seem to ignore it. I still tend to see her as that striking athletic woman who wore pants and never brought food to our family picnics. I believe she is delighted when she sees me and I move over to be with her.

"Do you always sit here?" I ask her.

"Yes," she answers me. "Carol and Billy (my cousin and her husband) might be coming with Eric (their son), but I don't know, with this weather. I know your Na-nan's still sick. And Toby (my godfather) probably came to early church. But yes," she tells me again, this time lifting an eyebrow as she looks at me, "this is where we all sit."

Before I can marvel at what homing instinct has guided me to this very pew, the music of the organ is swirling about the church air, cracking its stillness with jubilance. A procession of singers in bright purple robes, ministers in white—why aren't any of them women?—and altar boys—not girls, even yet?—carrying aloft a shimmering metal cross has swept forth from the rear of the church. Like a sharp gust of wind, we are all up and singing.

"A mighty fortress is our God, a trusty shield and weapon."

I worry about how many witches have been burned at the

stake, the flaming faggots at their feet ignited by Christians, yet my voice wants to rise for the sheer joy of singing along with the rest. Of course the key is not right for me — probably perfect for the damn men — so where I want to be strong, I must either force out a very low bass or sing very high. I am timid at first; but as I hear my aunt unfaltering beside me, I become bolder.

"The kingdom ours remaineth!" we sing in falsetto together.

We sit down and stand up and sit down and stand up again. The minister says, "Amen," and we say "Hallelujah," and he says "Hallelujah," and we say, "Amen." Every now and then we sing songs. It doesn't much matter. What matters is that everyone is here week after week, year after year, generation after generation trying to hold on to the same thing.

Like me in the bar on Saturday night.

When the minister begins his sermon, I know it's going to be about homosexuals burning in Hell and I'm frightened. Not about burning in Hell. I'm afraid that I'll have to stand up in front of God and everybody and say, "This is wrong. You wouldn't say Black people were going to burn in Hell if there were any out here in the congregation, now would you, even if you truly believed it? You might say, 'Get those Negroes out of here.' But I don't think you would just gloss over them like they didn't exist. So I want you to know, at least, that I am here and you're talking to me."

But what does this minister say? He says, "The topic of today's sermon is Freedom from Oppression."

Can you beat that?

I sat back ready to be challenged, enlightened or even enraged. I found myself lulled and confused. I noticed that I was scrutinizing the paint job on the ceiling, planning what I was going to do at work on Monday, trying to decide whether or not I should blow my nose in church. Just moments after the little girl sitting next to me started quietly singing Donna Summer songs to her doll, the minister granted us peace. Then we all began singing again and plates were passed out for money and cards that had been filled out by people who wanted to take communion.

The music deepened to a somber minor key. The minister ceremoniously held up wafers of Jesus and shot glasses of His blood given into death for my sins. This is the meat of it, I thought. Walking through fire. Handling snakes. Eating flesh.

I found myself waiting in line to kneel at the altar.

Maybe people like me are like Jesus, I thought, my knees on the carpet, my head bowed, my hands folded on the railing in front of me. We are people with burdens to carry, people who suffer abuse, people on whom anger is unleashed simply because we are who we happen to be. But we take it because we're stronger and maybe other people can't. We take it for them, for the earth, to help solve the problems. We absorb the evil of people who hate, to keep them from destroying everything else. Sometimes we hurt and some of us die, but that's just the way it has been. And then I thought that maybe that's what Jesus did when She died on the cross. That maybe that's what She continues to do every time She gives Her body for us to eat and Her blood for us to drink and I raised my head to receive Her.

This is my body.

No, the wafer did not sear a smoldering cross into the roof of my mouth. But the sweet blood red wine was in fact hot as it washed over my tongue and burned its way down my throat. It was as hot as that beautiful woman who had led an adoring procession of worshipers back and forth across a dance floor throbbing with music just the night before at the bar.

Can I buy you a drink?

I had been sitting on a stool with a glass of wine in my hand. "She looks familiar," I told a friend of mine who had friends of her own on the lookout to tell her when the woman would be passing by again so she could just look. She was that beautiful.

"Sure she looks familiar," she shouted to me over the music. "Probably from the cover of a magazine."

I pressed my fingertips lightly over my own face with its nose too big, cheeks too full. Sometimes I feel very sad that I am who I am and not someone for whom doors are opened more easily. Sometimes I feel bitter and angry that my life so far has not been such an easy one, and I wish for someone or something beyond me. Could I be wishing for the face of God? Could it be She with Whom I seek to commune week after week in the bar drinking wine with my friends?

Still the wine warms my belly as I kneel here at the altar with strangers who might hate or condemn me if they knew who I was yet I feel a sudden peace which passeth all understanding and I know that if there is not forgiveness around me, there is forgiveness within me. But how do I know that this feeling is God and not just a quick rush of sugar and alcohol from a fermented grape?

My aunt and I hugged goodbye in the parking lot outside of the church, letting ourselves be drenched together for a moment in the rain. I felt my muscles and bones beginning to ache. Our spirits filled with peace and acceptance, were we exposing our bodies for just a moment too long to a wrath of God pouring on Earth? Or was it only pouring on me standing outside of an umbrella of faith?

Now the storm is over, and here I am sick. My head is congested and it hurts and throbs if I bend down even just a little. My limbs are getting weaker and weaker. My nose is stopped up and I can hardly breathe. My skin feels hot. I'm getting cranky. I am cranky.

I'm not giving in.

I get on my bike. I lock my feet into the toe clips that are bolted to the pedals. I pull up with one leg and push down with the other. I slice through the air moving faster and faster. I stand up and push and pull harder. I come to an overpass. I take it on still standing up. My thighs begin to burn. My breathing is stabbing my chest. I make it to the top. I shift into my most efficient gear and, descending effortlessly, realize that I am almost flying, pushing into a wind that, I see more and more clearly, is not blowing from a storm outside of myself. As I hit the straightaway, each push and pull motion takes me further than I would have thought possible. I turn around and do it again.

I go to the pool. The water is colder than I would have liked. I'm still feeling miserably sick, but my body itself is growing stronger and stronger. I lift my left elbow, bring it up over my head, drop my hand, slightly cupped, fingers first into the water and stroke. I stroke again with my right arm, then my left arm, then my right, then I turn my head to the side while my left elbow is still in the air and I breathe. I kick, my legs held out straight, toes pointed, one two three kicks to each stroke. I follow the black line on the bottom of the pool back and forth until I realize that I'm breathing on every stroke and it still doesn't seem like enough air. I seem to be getting a chill. I give up and go into the sauna to sweat. To sweat out whatever evil is destroying me. And in one weakened moment, though my nakedness seems to be taking on a surprisingly somewhat beautiful form that I would never have thought could be mine, I'm afraid that everything I've been told is wrong with me is true. That I, in fact, was not welcome in God's house.

I decide to go home to my own house.

I think my lover and I should have sex.

Could she instead, she wants to know, fix me some hot apple cider sprinkled with fresh allspice, cloves, pieces of orange peel and cinnamon sticks in a thick ceramic mug?

No, it would be better if we had sex.

Could she, she asks me again, simply cradle me in the crook of her arm, hold the steaming mug to my lips and let its sweet liquid trickle gently down my throat?

I still think that we should have sex. But I reluctantly yield to her arms, her fruit drink and the dreamlike invitation of slumber. My head gives an involuntary jerk. My eyes open wide to click a final photograph of all that is around me. It blurs to but a pinhole of light and I am gone.

As quickly as that, I'm awake.

It is the moonlight on my face — or is it the dawn? No, what has wakened me is the sudden cessation of suffering. My breathing is no longer ragged. My head is clear and light. My muscles are vibrant with an energy I had believed was beyond me. My body and the body of this woman who loves me seem to be absorbing what brightness there is. We appear to be glowing with a light that could be coming from paradise. I could easily pull her to me, kneel before her and greedily drink from her persimmon lips now parted in open invitation. I lightly touch her sleeping face instead. Or is it my own that I stroke?

For breakfast, I mix in a blender a drink of fresh strawberries, an almost overripe banana, crushed ice and the juice of an orange that I squeeze myself in my U.S. Patented hand powered Juice-O-Mat, bought for 50¢ at a Lutheran Thrift Store where my mom sent me one time when I needed a sofa; and I drink it purely for the taste of it.

Could it really be so simple?

Of course not.

But in this moment, it is and I am.

I open my door to the brightness of this particular day, and I know that through it I will run well. I will run through hectic daily life and through peaceful fruit orchards and groves. I will run to Port and Burgundy and to simple red wine at the bar. I will run back and forth through sickness and storms into health and sunlight as naturally as a pendulum swings from one side to the other. I will run with strangers. I will run with my father, my aunt, my mother, my lover, the beautiful young woman on the dance floor. I will run with people who won't want to be running with me. I will enter a race. If I finish fiftieth, who will be forty-ninth? If I finish twelfth, who will be eleventh? If I finish first, who will be ahead of me? I stand on the threshold balanced on one leg, the other pulled behind me in a stretch. I find myself looking ahead, but I know that I'm already there.

The Healing

SANDY BOUCHER

*I*t was a great relief to go inside herself. Sheila worked with people who came bringing their aches and confusions, whose bodies she soothed with her touch. Lately she had been volunteering in a hospice, besides her usual work load, and the care for dying people drew upon her strength as no other endeavor had done. Twice a year she took off a week, said goodbye to friends and clients, and drove south in her battered pale-blue Valiant to the Mojave Desert to the meditation retreat given by Helga Brunt. Only once had she not gone, when the retreat had been scheduled for Passover week, the holiday she most loved to spend with her mother. It had been hard to give up that retreat, for Sheila, who was not usually susceptible to such enthusiasms, had over time developed a deep, steady admiration for Helga. We love those who give to us, and Sheila had received compassionate caring, wise guidance, and strict instruction in the practice of meditation from Helga. In gratitude, she gave herself to the rigorous schedule. There had never been a period in Sheila's thirty-five years when she had not worked hard; while some others at the retreat took walks out over the desert or slept through early morning meditation sessions, she plunged into the activities wholeheartedly, working even here.

But this retreat had begun badly. The morning before her

drive down from San Francisco she had backed into an open cabinet door, the metal corner scraping her flesh. The skin near her left shoulder was broken in a nasty cut that flamed now as she sat on her pillow in the meditation hall. For fifteen minutes Sheila had been trying to pay attention to the movement of breath in and out her nostrils; now she simply gave up, surrendering instead to the insistent throb of pain in her back.

Opening her eyes slightly, she saw the other sitters in the concrete-walled room. Men and women, mostly young, they sat very still and erect, or fidgeted as unobtrusively as possible. Looking past their shoulders, up to the place next to the tall wood bureau that served as an altar, Sheila squinted near-sightedly at the woman who sat facing the group. Helga's eyes were closed in her pale craggy face. This face looked as if it had been gouged at temple and cheek, where the flesh was sunken under the prominent bones. Time had carved it, stripping it to its essential contours. Helga was in her late fifties, but she might have been decades older, at moments any age at all.

Sheila thought back on her interview with Helga earlier today. "So you have this pain," Helga had said, her bright blue eyes fixing Sheila with fierce interest. "Is it unbearable?" In her thick German accent, the "r" sounded almost like a "w." (That accent still sometimes caused the hairs to rise on the back of Sheila's neck.)

"Unbearable?" Sheila repeated. And she considered. "No, I can bear it."

"Ah, good," Helga said, a sound not so much of approval as of acknowledgment. She smiled at Sheila. "I am not a stranger to pain myself. This hip of mine, since I broke it, is constant trouble."

Helga paused to look thoughtfully at Sheila for a few moments, and her face softened in sympathy. "But you," she said, "are you unhappy about this pain?"

Sheila shifted irritably. What the hell kind of question was *that!* Of course she was unhappy about it.

"Yes!" she said forcefully.

"I see," Helga murmured, nodding, and turned to speak to

another person in the room.

But when Sheila came back to the meditation hall and was once again immobile on her pillow, she heard the question again in her mind and understood why it had been asked. Apparently there might be more than one way to feel about the pain.

As she pondered this, the throbbing in her back increased and localized until it became a hard flaming knot. She drew in her breath, tears springing to her eyes, and held still, asking herself, Can I bear this?

The pain bit more deeply into her back, as if the flesh were gripped in jagged teeth. Sheila's thighs and upper arms twitched, her belly pulled back tightly. The hurt drew all her energy and made her its victim, driving every other thought from her mind.

Behind her someone coughed, mucus gurgling in his throat, and Sheila became aware of the other bodies in the room. Their proximity made her feel even more trapped.

Deliberately now, not in reaction but by her own volition, she sent her attention to the sensations in her back, and concentrated. The picture came to her of Helga when she had fallen a year ago in the dining room of the retreat and broken her hip. Helpless, she had lain on the floor all night, unable to move, until someone found her in the morning. How much more extreme that pain must have been than mine, now, Sheila thought. Then she saw the hands of a man in the hospice, the fingers clenched white-knuckled against physical torment more hideously all-encompassing than any she could imagine. Sheila was wracked with awareness of the pain of the dying people she tended. It was as if her body expanded to accommodate that agony, the pressure and weight of it straining inside her contours.

Now the tears that had stood in her eyes spilled over. She felt their warm wetness rolling down her cheeks, and she gave in to the crying. As she let grief take her, she clamped her lips together, trying to hold the sounds inside herself so as not to disturb the other meditators.

●

The desert spread out around her on every side to distant mountain ranges. This was the high desert, sandy soil dotted with creosote bushes and cat's claw, low greyish burrow-weed. Here and there a Mojave yucca raised its short spiky arms like a shamana over its humbler sisters. Humankind had made its mark, scattering small weathered houses like bits of debris across the flat expanse. But the desert had prevailed, and where people had fled before its insistent winds, its crushing heat, abandoned structures stood. Hinges, crusted with orange rust, squealed under the weight of a warped door, from which the veneer had lifted at top and bottom into brittle ruffles. Half-finished houses stood open to the sky, testament to the builders' foolishness or naïveté, their metal window casements whistling shrilly when the wind raked across them.

As Sheila walked out into the desert, she saw the houses tiny in the distance and could not tell which were lived in, which stood with empty windows. Near at hand was the pale crumbly earth, the bushes rising from it, each standing alone, tan and leafless now in winter. Sheila walked until she was some distance from the meditation hall. Then she stood still for a time, breathing deeply of the clear cold air. Her forward-tilting posture was born of nearsightedness. When she tried to know with her eyes, she pressed her head forward anxiously, a round head on which the hair stood springily in tight darkbrown waves, like the winter coat of a healthy animal.

Far out stood the first mountain range, a low brown jumble of rocks; beyond it, higher mountains rose slightly blue with haze. A storm was coming, Sheila knew, as she watched great black wedges of cloud advancing across the enormous empty arch of blue that was the sky.

Turning to look back toward the meditation hall, she saw Helga's long-skirted figure hurrying out the door. She began to do the walking meditation, lifting each foot carefully, moving it slowly forward and setting it down; and she thought of her struggle when she had first come to one of Helga's retreats. Sheila's parents viewed all Germans as monsters, and Sheila, while she had learned otherwise, still reacted with a swift surge of fear when she heard a German accent. She had grown up with stories of the concentration camps, her mother's sorrowing voice telling of the grandmother Sheila had never known, who had died on her way there, the uncles and aunts who had suffered horribly and lost their lives. Her mother and father had come to the United States from Germany before the war, but her mother told the stories as if she had been there, having heard them from the lone uncle who survived. To be Jewish, Sheila understood, was to hate Germans. She had been leery of Helga at first, distant and critical. She had asked the other Jewish students about their reactions, had heard them tell of Helga's skill as a teacher, her compassion. Sheila was drawn back again and again to meditate with Helga, and eventually she could not ignore Helga's wisdom and strong love for those around her. Despite her caution, at last she began to think of Helga's being German as an accident of fate for which the woman could not be held responsible.

Sheila put her foot down slowly, felt the weight of her body on her leg, moved forward, lifted her other foot. The wind played with her hair, dragging a lock across her forehead to tap at the lens of her glasses as she looked down at the delicate skeleton fingers of a bush clawing up from the dry earth. She flexed her own fingers, as if readying those small narrow hands to find the pressure point in a shoulder, to move an aching arm. For eight years now she had worked as a body therapist. When she had begun, at first studying Swedish massage, she had discovered a surprising aptitude in herself: surprising because before that she had lived chiefly above the neck, looking with a cold eye on anything "new age" or "touchy feely," and swiftly rejecting the intuitive or spiritual aspects of her own experience. The massage class had been a departure, a timid venture into strange territory. But after only a few lessons there had been no question in her that she had found what she was to do in this world. Later, as she studied Shiatsu and other techniques, and began to earn her living by applying them, she became extremely sensitive to the body's energy, able to respond to the subtle messages of flesh and bone. And the practice of meditation helped her deepen in her work.

A bright metallic call came in the brisk air. Here on the desert one could hear the conversation of people standing next to a house a hundred yards away. Sometimes the buzz of a motorbike ripped like an electric saw through the stillness; sometimes the boom of the weapons testing carried on by the air force at a nearby base opened great purplish balloons of sound that hovered above the ground for a few moments, then collapsed, disappeared. Now the gong sang out in tones like miniature rainbows.

Sheila looked up, seeing her fellow meditators turn in the direction of the meditation hall, begin to move slowly toward it. At its door she saw the maroon flash of Helga Brunt's long skirt, and her heart lifted.

•

At lunch the meditators sat on the floor in a circle around the bare dining room. Sheila leaned against the wall. "Remember," Helga said, "we are to remain mindful as we eat this food. Between each bite you will put down your utensil on the tray. You will pay attention to the taste and texture of the food, to the movement of your tongue." Sheila glanced up, seeing Helga lean forward holding her bowl of food before her as if she were offering it.

Chewing, Sheila thought that Helga herself was probably the only person among these well-fed Americans who had ever experienced hunger, for she had lived through the Second World War in Europe.

"Now, when you come to swallowing, attend to that. What kind of motion is it with your tongue, with your throat—is it several motions one after the other? Remember, we are eating now. We are not daydreaming or planning what we are going to do this afternoon." Helga chuckled. "Don't worry about this afternoon. I can tell you, we are going to sit some more. Let that happen when it happens. Now, you eat. *Know* that you are eating."

Swallowing, Sheila paid careful attention to the motions of

her throat. From Helga she had learned that each aspect of her existence was a proper object of investigation, and she was willing to attend to the most minute, subtlest experiences. When pursued with the rigor that Helga demanded, this investigation was the opposite of self-indulgence. Sometimes it brought Sheila to an awareness of her own body that was rending in its implications: experiencing the ache at the base of her tongue as she moved it against the insides of her cheeks, she felt the transiency of these collections of muscle and tissue and how little she could do to preserve them. Change, decay, the inevitable altering of matter from one form to another, became piercingly real to her, bringing her to a reverence for herself and other human beings.

It had taken Sheila several years to find a teacher who challenged and nurtured her, whose practice included service to the beings around her, including the animals. There were always one or two people in great mental or emotional difficulty whom Helga was sheltering at her retreat center; always some stray dogs, whom Helga cared for meticulously. Sheila saw the generosity with which Helga met each human being, fully acknowledging her or him, showing no hint of judgment no matter who the person might be or how he or she was acting.

Now in the dining room, Helga directed the kitchen volunteers in serving second helpings. They were led by Michio, her Japanese assistant, a small thin man with hair stiff and straight as a shoebrush. He was one of the students who lived with Helga and were in training to be teachers themselves. Fussily Helga whispered to him, telling him to dip the ladle *this* way, taking his hand to show him how. Sheila smiled, watching, thinking how very human and fallible Helga was in this officiousness. It made her familiar, like Sheila's only surviving aunt, Aunt Bella, who when Sheila visited always brought out borscht and challah and pickled herring, which she insisted Sheila eat, whether she was hungry or not, and followed up with crumbly strudel, shoving plate after plate at her. In her austerity Helga was as aggressive as Bella in her liberality.

Michio inclined his head to Helga, allowed her to grip his hand and move it. Sheila admired his composure: she knew she would have been irritated in that situation, might even (she hoped not) have jerked her hand away. It was often in watching Michio that Sheila recognized how far she had to go to develop the calm acceptance she sought.

•

Walking to the meditation hall after lunch, Sheila shivered. The air had grown much colder; there was a wetness to it that pierced through her clothes to send her skin rippling. It felt like the air in Michigan, where she had grown up, just before a snow. Looking up, she saw that the clouds had eaten up the blue, spreading and merging to form a swollen grey roof above her. Sometimes snow fell on the high desert, she had heard, but she had not expected to witness that phenomenon. The wind pushed at her clothes as she stopped at the door of the meditation hall to take off her shoes.

Inside, some people were already settled. Others arranged their shawls and scarves about them. The hall was unheated, the air cold against cheeks and hands, and everyone wrapped up before each sitting. Sheila took off her glasses, tucked her blanket around her back and legs.

She closed her eyes, making herself as quiet as possible, hoping to sink deep to that peaceful place. Attending to her breathing, she felt the in-breath through her nostrils, the instant's pause at the end of the breath, and then the air going out. Again and again, until she opened to that undersea place like the far reaches of the sky, that silence lighter and more palpable than any she knew in ordinary life. For a time she rested there, allowing herself simply to be, asking nothing but this moment, while knowing that soon the pain in her back would begin to sharpen.

She was not aware that Helga had entered the meditation hall until she heard the bell, and opened her eyes to see Helga seated at the front, smiling roguishly.

"Stand up now," Helga ordered. "We are going to do some

stretches here to work out all those kinks you got."

As they shuffled about, folding their blankets, rising on their stiff legs, a voice cried, "Look, it's snowing!"

All eyes turned to the window, beyond which the snowflakes fell like flecks of light against the grey air.

Helga chuckled. "So it is snowing. There is absolutely nothing we can do about it. Let's do our exercises!"

As Sheila glanced back at her, she saw Helga push herself up from her stool, pause for an instant, her jaw clamped tight. Helga took a long breath and slowly straightened, pushing against the pain in her hip, and Sheila realized that her own body had tensed in sympathy.

At Helga's direction, Sheila and the others bent and twisted and stretched, easing their tight muscles. Then Helga had them sit down again and she began to talk. Clearly she was in a buoyant mood.

When she told an anecdote from her childhood, Sheila became uneasy. It was unusual for Helga to speak of her background. She lived very much in present time, and drew her teaching examples generally from incidents that had occurred no earlier than yesterday. Sheila did not like being reminded that Helga had grown up in Germany.

"You know, when people think of Germany during the war, they think only of the atrocities. The Nazis they see as beasts. But there is something of value. Yes, it is true. There was a deep spiritual training incorporated in the Nazis' teachings."

Sheila gripped her hands before her.

"This is something totally ignored, totally forgotten," Helga continued. "I know about it myself because I was a member of the Hitler Youth, where that training was pursued. We learned to revere nature, we honored ... a dimension ... other than the material. I tell you, in everything there is some wholesome element."

Sheila had stopped breathing several moments before.

Pushing her glasses up on her nose, she leaned to peer at Helga. In perfect unconsciousness of the effect of her words, Helga sat looking serenely out over the group.

"It was there that I got my first inkling of ... how shall I say ... the interconnectedness of all beings."

The Hitler Youth! Sheila's stomach lurched. After college, compelled by a strange urgency, she had toured Northern Germany while on a European bike trip. Now she sees before her the groups of khaki-clad boys who would come marching into the youth hostels. Sheila had stared at them with horrified fascination, thinking, They're just like the Hitler Youth! Their presence set off in her mind the voices of her parents, the grainy documentaries seen in her European history classes.

Helga had moved now to some other subject, leaving Sheila paralyzed.

She sat through the rest of Helga's remarks and the half-hour meditation with her mind stretched wide, dazed. Had no one else heard those words? she wondered, and opened her eyes to look around, staring at the faces of the people she knew to be Jewish. Why had there not been a response in the room? No one had gasped, not even Sheila. Nor had she raised her hand to demand, "What do you *mean?* What did you just *say* to us!"

Helga sat before them, eyes closed, hands limp in her lap. Sheila stared at her face. The shadowed eye sockets, the jut of cheekbone seemed cruelly sculptured now into harsh hollows and protuberances. The mouth looked sunken, impervious. The eyes had disappeared. Sheila gazed at the face while Helga's words pounded in her brain.

•

The others were pacing slowly in meditation near the hall, but Sheila had set off in a quick walk across the desert. Going out of the hall, she had turned her face away from Helga, but the woman's image was there in her nevertheless, taunting her. The snowflakes touched Sheila's face with cold fingertips and sat like tiny white spiders on the lenses of her glasses. Through them she saw the distant mountains toward which she strode, her feet thumping angrily on the ground, her body tilted forward in a headlong rush.

The desert had softened as snow swept across it dimming the

outlines of distant houses and clinging like new fluffy foliage to the skeletal bushes. In the hollow of each long spine of a yucca plant, a neat wedge of snow lay cradled. As if with a sigh of relief, the desert soil and plants gave themselves to the wet silent caress of the snow.

Sheila paced among the bushes, a brutal hurrying force in this gentle landscape. Trudging forward, she passed the exposed concrete floor of a house, on which rested an iron bed, the coils of its springs delicately limned with snow.

Hitler Youth! It had been children who led the Gestapo to her family. The daughter and son from the household next door had seen movement through the dusty window at the back of the drygoods store in Bremen where Sheila's uncles and aunt and grandparents were hidden. The children, trained by the Hitler Youth to note anything suspicious, had reported their find and stood watching as the Gestapo kicked open the back door of the shop and dragged out the terrified people.

Only her Uncle Zed and Aunt Bella had emerged from the concentration camps alive, and had come to the United States afterward. When Sheila was born, her parents saw her as the cherished issue of a devastated family, the child whose new life would burn like a flame to commemorate those other lives that had been lost.

When she was old enough to understand, her parents told her she was a Jew but that it was best not to talk about that with her friends at school. (They were only the third Jewish family to have settled in their town.) They spoke to her of the deaths of her grandmother and Uncle Reuben, Aunt Doris, little Felix who was only fifteen at the time. Sheila did not want to hear. She began to have nightmares as the terror crept in on her, and in her growing up she was dark and shy, not even trying to win the acceptance of her WASP schoolmates, embarrassed for her mother, whose clothes were never right, whose hair was a black wiry bush, who spoke with an accent.

It was not until a few years ago that Sheila had wanted to know about her family's experience in Nazi Germany. Her father was dead now. On a visit to her mother, she asked to hear the story she had so vigorously fought not to hear during all her growing up. At first her mother would not talk, turned stubbornly away, saying, "Ach, only *now* you want to hear all this! I don't want to tell it. Why bring up this suffering?" But Sheila persisted, and finally her mother told the story. The names, the places flowed from her as if it had happened yesterday, and as she described the death of her own mother, as Zed had told her about it, in a boxcar where people lay head to thigh, where ice covered the cracks in the walls, her face took on a look that Sheila remembered from her childhood. She had seen it often then, that lost, stunned expression, her mother's eyes deep and vulnerable. Her mother described the conditions in the camp where her father and her brothers had died in the gas chambers, and her sister Doris had been killed by a guard. Sheila thought she could not bear more of this story, she wanted her mother to stop, but the voice went on. They sat late into the night, the woman emptying all of it out for Sheila to know.

On her mother's face now, in Sheila's mind, there appeared the features of Helga, a superimposition of Germanic starkness on her mother's round cheeks and mouth. The two women were near the same age, Sheila realized. They had grown up in the same country. How horrifying it was to know for sure that Helga had been on the side of the murderers. Her image now had grown in brightness, causing the round troubled face of Sheila's mother to fade. Sheila bent forward, hugging her arms to her chest. What was she to do with this weight like a jagged rock turning in her chest?

•

"But Sheila, I did not mean to upset you. I was pointing out a lesson, only."

Sheila flexed her hands, shook her head viciously. "How can you speak of *value* in relation to ..." she struggled for words.

They were seated in Helga's tiny stuffy room behind the dining room, Sheila on the bed, Helga in an armchair pulled close. Sheila hunched over, not six inches from Helga's knees.

She could remember each of the times she had sat here previously, bringing her confusion or her pain to be soothed.

"I see I have hurt you."

"That's not the point! To link spiritual training to Naziism! To talk so casually about belonging to the Hitler Youth! How can you even admit you were a part of that!"

"Oh Sheila, my being in the Hitler Youth had nothing to do with the awful crimes. We were children. I lived in a little village, and we girls in our group made wreaths of flowers, and decorated our hair. We danced in the meadows, we floated down the river on rafts and dove in. It was harmless, my dear, it was ... nature and ... and Old Germany."

Sheila stared uncertainly at her. She understood that it was this nature worship, this exhuming of ancient gods and traditions that had led, by inexorable cause and effect, to the murder of her grandparents, uncles, aunts and millions of leftists, gypsies, Jews, homosexuals and other "misfits"; yet Helga's recital of sylvan gambols was delivered so ingenuously that Sheila almost believed in her innocence.

Helga's look changed to worry. "How can I convince you I am not ... condoning ... the Nazis' actions. I was a young girl. We had no knowledge of the camps. I was trying only to point out that even in the most ... corrupt ... of situations there may be something ... wholesome ... pure...."

Shcila sat in angry confusion. She did not want Helga to apologize for her childhood or her ideas. What she wanted, she realized, was for Helga to *know how she felt*. And something more. What was it?

"Barbara came to me too," Helga said, "and Jon, and told me they are Jewish, and Carla and Betty who said they are not Jewish themselves ... they said my remarks were offensive to them. I am trying to understand."

"Why is it so goddamned hard to understand!" Sheila flashed out. "Millions died ..." and she cut off her words.

Helga drew back from Sheila's fury, her lips trembling. "Please control yourself," she said. "You act as if I ..."

"Oh ... oh ..."Sheila clasped her hands before her and shook

109

her head slowly back and forth. I'm not getting through to her, she thought, I'm not doing this well ... She struggled to still the shaking of her arms. "I think I have to go now, Helga."

•

After dinner, Sheila drew Jon and Barbara aside, and they went out to stand shivering in the night to talk. Jon, who was an accountant from Los Angeles, began to analyze the collective state of mind of the German people before the war. Barbara, hurt and upset, pointed out that at the December retreat last year Helga had spoken of Christmas rituals and beliefs and had never mentioned Chanukah. Sheila remembered, then, the retreat that had been thoughtlessly scheduled for Passover week. As Barbara raged against the tyranny of Christmas, the bell rang calling them to meditation. They hesitated, looking to each other. Jon touched Sheila's hand. "Tomorrow let's talk more. We'll find a time." Then, with awkward abruptness, Barbara put her arms around both their shoulders, and for a few moments they were holding each other, leaning into the warmth of each others' bodies. Sheila, her face pressed into the wool of Jon's coat, fought the tears that swelled behind her eyelids.

•

The meditation hall was like a cave at night, its cinderblock walls touched by the soft light of candles, its ceiling dark. Sticks of incense smoked on the altar, sending out an odor of oranges, cloves, musk, to encircle the sitters and draw them together in a single intention. Flanked by masses of red and white carnations, a statue of the buddha sat in meditation. The gleaming wood surfaces of his chest and forehead held the candle glow; his closed eyelids were like the curved petals of flowers; his mouth was sensuously full. His form seemed the embodiment of stillness, graceful and rounded at shoulder, knee; sweetly androgynous; as peaceful as a stone.

Near him, in a pool of light cast by a ceiling bulb, Helga prepared to give her nightly lecture. The meditators sat on their pillows, most with closed eyes, composed faces, to listen, but Sheila had left her glasses on this time: her eyes were open, watching Helga.

"In our lives, you know, we rush about, we have so much pressure. You with your jobs, your families, your speeding on the freeways ... it causes our muscles to tighten, our bodies to become hard. That is why, when I guide you in meditation, I take you to your bellies, to your mouths, to your diaphragms ... to plunge you inside your bodies and soften them."

Sheila had been drawn here by the anguish alive in her chest, by the faith that this teacher could point the direction out of pain, even pain caused by herself. She looked to where Jon sat, still as the buddha on the altar. Barbara was nowhere to be seen.

"We have to help you to know your livingness, to *experience* this body where you are inside it all the time and you know nothing about it. To know what is real, we must begin with our most gross manifestation, the body, before we begin to go on and consider our feelings or our thoughts."

Sheila watched Helga, who looked gracious and relaxed now in her blouse with its full white sleeves, whose head was covered with a rose-colored scarf this evening. Helga smiled as she talked, her blue eyes searching the faces of her listeners. Now she chuckled.

"Do you even know, right now, that you are sitting? Feel for a moment the weight of your body pressing down on the pillow. Say to yourself, I am sitting, and feel the sensations of it. That is what is real right now, isn't it? Hmmm? And so you touch this reality of your body which is sitting."

She didn't get it, Sheila thought, looking at Helga's cheerful face shadowed at the gaunt eye sockets and cheekbones. She's just the same as before. She really didn't hear the trouble she caused. Helga is a spiritual teacher, Sheila told herself, one who has cleared her mind so that she can see *what is:* how then can she be so blind to this? She looked down at her hands in her lap, resentful.

But soon, as Helga fell silent and the meditation period

started, Sheila began to see the faces of her parents' few friends, humble frightened people newly arrived from Europe, who came to spend Sabbath or celebrate the holidays, who talked of their difficulties in adjusting to this new life. How different it was when Sheila went to the university, where she would visit her best friend Rhonda at the Jewish sorority. The girls there were slim and magazine-ad pretty; they wore expensive clothes and talked loudly of the vacations their parents would send them on for the holidays, and they treated Sheila as if she were invisible. Among them she felt even more dark and foreign-looking than she felt among gentiles. They seemed to know exactly how to *be* in the world, as if this university belonged to them. While she took a holiday job wrapping boxes in the store in which her father sold shoes, they went to Bermuda, or to Colorado to ski. She hated them for making her envy them. She hated them for treating her as if she didn't exist.

•

That night Sheila lay on her cot in the little cottage that housed the women. Confusion kept her from sleep. How could she put it together, her gratitude to Helga and her anger at Helga? It disturbed her that tonight she had watched the woman's pain in getting up and not cared, even felt some satisfaction that Helga suffered. She was astonished that she could have come so far from the day before, when she had put her head to the floor and cried for the pain of all creatures.

I hate her for being a lousy German, Sheila thought. I hate her for speaking of spirituality and the Nazis in the same breath. She stared up into the darkness, clenching her jaws, gripping her hands together across her chest. She saw the faces of Zed and Bella, the old brown photograph of her grand-mother's face. The hatred came up sour in her mouth, and with it the memory of the brash blond WASP children in the schools she attended. How weird they thought she was, if they noticed her at all. Mostly she had slunk away from their arrogance, but at moments rage had flamed up in her at some particularly brutal slight and she had wanted to hurt and humiliate them.

Sheila curled tightly into a ball and pressed the heels of her hands against her eyes. She felt trapped, tied here on the bed by the fury pulsing in her. She judged it ugly, and hated herself for letting it take her over so completely, yet she could not escape its grip.

●

Someone was pushing at her arm, making her body rock in the bed. Sheila jerked away from the touch, turned to see the skinny form bent over her.

"Come outside," he whispered. "I want to ask you a favor."

And he was gone.

Had his presence been real? she asked herself. But no, she had felt his hand on her arm, dimly seen the bristles of hair standing up on his head.

Sheila sat up and put on her sweater. She got out of bed, slipped on her sweatpants, felt around on the low table for her glasses, put them on, and threaded her way through the sleeping bodies to the door.

Michio stood at the corner of the building. He was like a shadow in the moonlight, so thin and still. Sheila shivered, feeling the cold on her thighs and shoulders, as she walked toward him. Snow still lay on the ground, a gleaming silver coverlet.

"It's Helga," he said, leaning close to Sheila. "Tonight the pain is very bad. Since you do massage, I thought you would be able to help her."

Sheila might have laughed. At this moment she felt more like a cornered animal than a human being capable of helping someone. She stared in indecision at Michio's smooth face.

"Does *she* want me to?"

"Oh, you know how she is. She doesn't want to take the time. But it's worse tonight. *I'm* asking you to help her."

"Well ..." How could she say no? How could she go back in and lie on her cot? Sleep was impossible anyway. Her anger turned on Michio. Why didn't he mind his own business! Sheila looked at the ground, at Michio's feet in worn boots. She did not possess the strength of will to refuse him.

"Let me get my coat."

In the thick darkness of the cottage, Sheila stood for a moment over her bed, seeing Michio in her mind. With a weird clarity she saw him both as himself and as a "Japanese," and she wondered what he felt about the people of this nation that had dropped the bomb on people like him. Did hatred like hers bubble in his insides, ready to boil over? Did he, as himself right here and now, even think about such things, or was it just her guilt that made her lump him with the victims?

•

They walked down the road in the still night, under a waning moon that stood high in the sky. All the shadows were sharp against the snow, slicing dark from light, plunging the mind from gleaming surface to bottomless blackness, and back, in a motion that was disorienting and thrilling. Ahead was the dining hall, crouched low like a stalking animal, one golden eye peering out as if searching the night for prey. That would be the window of Helga's room.

When Michio and Sheila entered the warm, crowded room, Helga glanced up from the desk. Her eyeglasses had slid down on her nose, and she peered over them, a startled blue gaze.

"Who's this you've brought?!"

Michio stood at the doorway with his cap in his hands. "I asked Sheila to come ... to see if she can relieve some of your pain."

"What nonsense!" Helga threw down her pen on the papers. "She should be sound asleep. Go back right now and go to sleep, Sheila."

"Michio tells me you're suffering a lot from your hip," Sheila said in the level voice she used with clients.

"Yes, and so what. We won't change it. It comes from that metal brace they put in."

Sheila glanced at Michio, who gave her a pleading look.

"We can relieve it a little," she said. "You need sleep too, Helga."

Helga grimaced. "Ah, you are still angry with me for what I

said today, you want to torment me."

Was that supposed to be a joke? Sheila wondered, but she saw no amusement in Helga's face, only a stiff, defended expression. Sheila brought her cold hands from her pockets and rubbed them together.

"A few minutes, Helga. It'll relax you...."

"You are forgetting, here I have all these bills to attend to, and a stack of letters to answer."

"Please," Michio said, "now that Sheila is awake."

"Hmmm." Helga pursed her mouth and stared down at the papers on her desk. "Well, if I cannot get rid of you...."

Michio left the room. Sheila helped Helga out of her skirt, surprised at the flower-patterned long underwear she wore under it.

"Do I have to take off my BVD's?" Helga asked, her eyes sparking.

Sheila laughed abruptly. "You can leave them on if you like."

As she watched Helga lie down on the bed, she felt utterly helpless, as if she would not be able to raise her arms.

"Michio worries about me too much," Helga said.

"I want to ask you to be quiet, Helga. Just pay attention to what you feel, just relax into it."

Sheila placed both hands over Helga's hip and simply held them there, trying to concentrate. But she was weirdly disrupted, wondering what she was doing here, her body pulling back violently from the flesh she touched.

She lifted her hands from Helga's hip.

"Give me just a little time to get ready," she said. "Guess I'm still sleepy."

She turned away from the bed. Clasping her hands before her, she closed her eyes. How can I possibly do this? she asked herself, feeling how rigidly sullen her body stood, how anger coursed in the muscles of her arms.

"Sheila, there is no need. Really." Helga's voice came, and Sheila heard the deep weariness in it. "Dear, you go back to bed and I will get on with my work."

Sheila turned to her. Looking at Helga on the bed, she could see how her body drew in to protect her injured hip. The shoulders tensed, the legs and arms contracted; all the muscles of her trunk drew tight and locked. Sheila saw this in ripples of energy. She saw the pulsing center of the pain in Helga's hip. Looking at Helga's body, she understood somewhere in herself that this was a human being who suffered. The awareness simplified her intention, but did not dull the intensity that rode her shoulders down and burned within her belly like a banked fire.

Without a word, she put her hands on Helga's hip and held them there, closing her eyes. She waited to feel the strength that came from her solar plexus. Her fingers read the distress in the muscles of Helga's hip.

Helga was silent. Soon Sheila could sense her surrendering, and she felt the responsibility shift to her. And in those few moments her love for Helga rose up to flame with a bright heat that caused her cheeks to flush. This woman who had given her so much: whom she raged against. How could she hate and love so strongly at the same time. Sheila turned her face away, blinking back tears, until she could suffer the feelings without betraying them.

She lifted one hand and placed it on Helga's knee, keeping her other hand on the hip. She let the potency caught in the damaged hip move down the leg to the knee, connecting the two joints, dissipating the tension. Then she moved to place one hand on the knee and the other on Helga's ankle, to draw that force down into the foot. And at last she spread her arms wide to hold hip and ankle, distributing the energy evenly throughout the leg.

Helga lay still, her eyes half open, submitting to Sheila's touch, and Sheila, scalded by what she felt, worked on. She had not imagined there could be such pain in this; she willed herself to face it all, and not to let it interfere with the steady caring her hands gave.

Gently, Sheila helped Helga turn over, and began work on the backs of her thighs. She found the pressure points to relieve the tension in thighs and lower back. By this time she was excruciatingly aware of the body before her and her own body with its broad shoulders, its short strong arms, the faint vestige of pain still there in her own back. She saw with unnatural clarity her small hands white in the lamplight on the ridiculous flowered cotton that covered Helga's thighs. Sheila pressed steadfastly on two points just above the knees.

"Does that release?" she asked softly.

Helga sighed. "Oh, it is marvelous. A great relief." Her scarf had slipped back from the grey-blond hair knotted under it. Her hands lay open-palmed on the bedspread.

With great care, Sheila began to work on the lower leg, the ankle, the foot, knowing this would open up the hip joint and cause Helga to have sensation in her whole leg.

Time moved very slowly. Sheila worked with a rapt face, her lips held lightly together, her eyes closed much of the time. She did not think out her next move, consciously choose from the many techniques she had mastered in the last eight years. Instead, she responded to the body's needs, letting it lead her to the next place of touch, aware of her own physical being in relation to this one, as if they leaned together in space, weight against weight, balancing. And deep inside this concentration, where the burning ate into her flesh, the questioning began again. What exactly do I want from Helga? What could she do to make this better? And she realized she wanted Helga to admit to her complicity, as a German, in the horrors of the war, as Sheila had had to admit to her own envy and aversion and fear. This Helga had not done. And what if she never did it?

Sheila remembered the retreat last year when a man in his sixties had fallen ill. Helga had moved him immediately from the bunkhouse to the bedroom of the house. She had called the doctor, and then had proceeded to tend the man, going in and out of his room with basins and towels and cups of tea. Getting up to go to the outhouse in the middle of the night Sheila had seen Helga hurrying across the windswept yard, her skirt flapping, a bottle of medicine in her hand, her face steadfast and gentle. At any hour of day or night Helga made herself available to her students, who were always welcomed when they knocked at her door. She drew no boundaries between herself and another's need.

Sheila worked on the sound leg and hip, knowing that it had been compensating for the other. She massaged Helga's back, and finally her shoulders, for in order to protect the hip Helga brought the tension and demands of movement into her upper body. Sheila thumbed the tendons of Helga's neck to loosen them, looking down into the large-boned face that had taken on a sweet childlike expression about the eyes and mouth.

Helga was asleep.

•

As she came out of the dining hall, Sheila looked up into the pale, open sky. Toward the horizon hung the moon, astonishingly large, transparent, apricot-tinted, poised just above a small clump of rocks. This swollen moon was disturbingly like a mirage there above the desert. In the opposite direction the bright globe of the sun rose in orange splendor.

Sheila turned away from this drama to sit on the step and look down at the brilliant snow. As she had last night, once again she determined that she must leave. She saw herself packing her few belongings, getting in her car. But what of Barbara and Jon, what of the two gentile women who had gone to talk to Helga? What was it that had made all of them go to Helga rather than run away from her?

A scraping sound caused her to look up. There next to the shed, Michio was feeding the dogs. As he bent and poured the food into the metal bowls, then set the bag of dogfood on the ground, each of his gestures was clean, thoughtful, standing almost outside of time, as if these actions were the most crucial in the universe. But who could know what was going on in his head, Sheila thought. Maybe he's fantasizing about his girlfriend, if he has one; maybe he's craving a cheeseburger; maybe he's having a mental argument with Helga. And she found herself grinning at the possibilities. Nobody escapes being a human being, she thought. Nobody.

As she got up to go back to the sleeping cottage, she knew she would stay, but later this day, after she had slept, she would talk with Barbara and Jon again, and with Carla and Betty; she would ask them to go as a group with her to meet with Helga. Perhaps if they spoke carefully enough, and together, Helga would understand them. Perhaps she would open herself to the experience of these people who were her students.

Sheila kicked her feet in the snow, feeling exhausted and loose in her body, suddenly aware that there remained only the barest shadow of discomfort in her back. The pain was gone, leaving a faint tingling in her flesh.

Sticktalk

VICKIE L. SEARS

I was walking alone through a coastal village feeling lonely and pensive. Glad to be on a reservation. That in itself made it safer for many feelings and perhaps riddle answers to recent puzzlings. I was thinking about going to the Shaker ceremony in the morning. It had been a long time since I had participated in any ceremonies other than pow-wows. I'd been living in the city for almost three years. A concrete-caught citizen far away from the smell of sweat lodges with water-splashed spitting rocks. Missed the sounds and smells of old ways ceremonies.

It seemed especially important at this time because I had been reminiscing about drinking for weeks. There was struggle staying sober. I'd been sober for eleven years. Even recently celebrated that anniversary but the wall of protection seemed fragile. Almost every recent day my mind tongue tasted the bitter heat of scotch. I salivated. It seemed real again. That getting drunk would make everything better. All the world issues and ordinary life problems would fade to oblivion. Nothing would hurt. I would have control of my environment again. Fool's talk on a fool's walk. Splurges of dirges, I mused.

I passed broken window houses. Abandoned trailers. Homes with woodpiles and bicycles in the yard. Odd piles of beer cans and bottles. I didn't want to think about what the rate of alcoholism might be in the village. Didn't want to be reminded of a major disease of my people. Or myself. Those were social worker's thoughts. Images of internalized oppression and all. I was supposed to be resting. Began to cry, when I heard an Elder voice on the wind.

"Come down to the beach. Come past the lighthouse along my long beach. We'll meet."

I probably imagined it but decided to see the lighthouse anyway. Walked past the Tribal buildings which were Saturday empty. Skirted over logs around the lighthouse. Heard waterwaves rub rocks over each other. Saw children running in the foam in summersun on the winter's day. Smelled clams and kelp cooking. Stared at the giant out-cropped rocks before turning south on the beach. The tide was full and curling across the sand. Up and down I traversed logs, tires and heaps of floating kelp. It was cold. Clear.

The beach at this village has spirits all about. I felt them in windbrushes of ancient songs. The night before had been filled with fires, drums and dancing. I had seen the dead ones in circles of dance. Could feel them all around me now. I walked slowly, feeling their power. Wondered if I had been a coastal native in some past life or if those of other worlds just spoke to all people of all tribes. Just then a Stick rose up to speak. It was red, brown and yellow, nearly five feet long and waving itself in front of me. I stopped, both fearful and not.

"Squadelich?" I asked. "Medicine Stick?"

It didn't speak. It fell, quite flat, into the sand. I walked closer. Didn't touch it. Bent down to examine it more thoroughly.

"I called you to come. You did that well, but you didn't recognize me," came an indignant response.

With that, I sat on the nearest log and waited. The Stick was quiet for a time. I looked toward the sea. I didn't find it strange to be waiting on stickspeaking. My father had repeatedly proven, when I was a child, that all things have their own spirits and lessons to share. I am just as the sticks and rocks. I may not always know my purpose, but it will be clear to me when I need to know. I will behave just as I am supposed to at that moment. Rocks had taught me before. Children. Adults. Animals. The burning of sweet grass. Many things. So I logsat, cold in winterwind waiting for this Stick to speak.

Stick began to hum. The song seemed familiar. I rocked. After a time, the Stick raised itself on a jagged leg. Rested on its side.

"Peaceful here, aay?"

"Yes, Stick."

"Feels good, aay?"

"Yes, Stick."

"Not like the other place where you live?"

"No, Stick."

"You cannot just run to hide here forever."

"True, Stick."

"What do you want here?"

"I don't know. I feel confused. Can't find direction for a lot of things."

"If you return to swallowing you will lose all of you."

I didn't respond. I knew what that Elder was talking about, but hadn't completely given up thoughts of drinking. I didn't look at the Stick.

It flipped off its leg and rolled toward the surf across the flat beach.

"If you don't follow you'll never have the answer!" it yelled.

My mind said, "The hell with you Stick. You're just a fantasy anyway. I'm not going to rescue you. Go away."

The Stick rolled over and over on itself until it reached the edge of the receding tide. It stood straight up and twirled itself in the sand. Slight stroking ripples surrounded the Stick but never strong enough to dislodge it from the root it made for itself. Now it wasn't a matter of saving the Stick. I could no longer view water, cliffs or seagullsailing without that Stick being in the periphery of my vision.

I moved down the beach a few feet never looking back at the Stick. It was silly to be paying attention to a Stick. Calling it an Elder. The conflicts of old beliefs and part city-rearing pushed at me. I sat down on a big log and began to explore my new territory. Then I saw the Stick tangled in the rubble of a new batch of debris. It was grinning at me! I looked back to where I had been and the Stick wasn't there.

"Not there, aay?"

"Old Stick, if you are not a medicine teacher, who are you? You seem like a person of magic. I know nothing of magic."

"Medicine sticks come to those who know them. I am not medicine. I am not magic. Take me home with you."

"Stick, you're teasing me and I'm too old for your game."

The Stick did not respond. I sat a while, listening. Heard nothing. Decided again I was being foolish. I began to walk up a path away from the beach. I stopped. Puzzled. Perhaps I should go back to the Stick. Maybe I'd forgotten how to listen. I rounded a corner and saw the Stick again. The Old One was now resting against a fat log way above high tideline right next to the path. It hummed as I neared. I smiled. Stopped. Listened. Finally said, "Old Stick, what do you think people will say if I tell them I'm out talking to a piece of wood?"

The Stick stopped singing. Fell flat. Made no noise. After a long pause, I started to walk away. Suddenly that Stick sprang in front of me. I jumped back.

"Ashamed of your knowing yourself inside of you? Aaaay, Ha!"

Stick threw itself across the path. I tried to raise my leg over it, but there was a wall surrounding its body. I had to walk back to the beach, going a long ways down it, to find another path back to the motel.

It was late afternoon when I reached the motel. I took a chair and book out to the balcony, looked on the sea, and watched the sun softly sink towards the water. I saw people come and go along the path where the Stick still stationed itself. Throughout the evening, they walked down to the beach to make fires. The melting marshmallows with their thick sweetness thinning out the air. Laughter mixing with the crackles of windwoven salal leaves and songs that echoed over ancient windweaving melodies. Low and permanent singing. Forever there from the land ancestors. From the people living there now. There was no solid sleep for me that night. My dreams were filled with faces of people I didn't remember. 1 saw the Stick being used as a bat by a ballbouncing child; the Stick being held by an old, old woman. The Stick dancing. Singing. Calling to me.

In the early pale-green morning light I went down the beach-path. The Stick was still laying there. I sat next to it. Its sun-stroked streaks were shiny rich in colors. Maroon swirls. Ocher slashes. Mahogany rivulets running to a sepia strain that slid into whitegray. A yellow eye that curled into a cocoa grin. Tentatively, I stretched my left finger onto the grin. Heard a giggle. I followed an umber stripe down the Stick's body. Heard myself sing some song that must have come from my Grandmother. Surely it wasn't mine. The Elder began to hum. Asked, "Will you take me home now? We have things to do together."

I answered, "Old Stick, you live on the beach. You won't like it in the city! There's lots of noise, bad smells and many sad sad people. It's got too many lights. It eats my time away and chews up my soul. You won't like it."

The Stick said, "Not all things are bad. Take me home with you."

I sighed. Said, "Alright, Old One."

Stick said, "You can step over me now."

With hesitation, I extended my leg over the Stick and stepped across. Then Stick stood up beside me, letting out a sharp long trill as I put my hand on top of her head. She had seemed much taller before. Now she was precisely the right length as a walking stick.

Walking with the Stick, I continued down the path to the beach, listening to the winds and filling myself with the sea-smells before returning to the motel and packing the car. As I started to put the Stick into the trunk of my car she let out a cry.

"Aaay? Would you like to ride in that darkness? Put me in the front, next to you. With something soft beside me. I want to rest on a pillow."

I put the Old One next to the front seat with a rolled-up sweater by her side. I packed the car and we drove away through the big trees. Lost the ocean sounds. Heard howling of wind funneled between hills, echoing on the water of a mountain lake.

"That's a lovely lake," Stick said. "Stop the car! Listen to that singing!"

I did. Sat in the tree wind. In the cold. In its warm. Felt the softness. Got back in the car and drove the long way to the ferry with wind in my ears.

On the ferry, the Elder asked to be taken to the side railing. I was holding her tightly when the Old One said, "You can't possess anything but yourself. Let me loose!"

She easily balanced herself. Swayed to the thump thump thump thump thump thump of the waterslapping flat bottomed ferry. I stood awed by her delicate dance. Looked about to see if anyone else watched. No one saw. The Elder said, "Aaaay. Don't look about. It's all in you. Everything you need to dance yourself."

I asked, "What's that mean, Old Stick?"

Stick's answer was, "We're docking. Put me back."

The Elder was silent the rest of the way home. When we arrived, the Old One said, "Put me by the front door."

I put her there where she is poised to leap at me. That Elder with her head howling at the ceiling, screams to be remembered for her ancient nature.

In the days that have followed she has poked at me with teasing, questions or statements obliquely made.

"Your work is too much," she once intoned.

"Night is for sleep," she charges.

"Ceremony is always," she warns.

One day she asked, "Why did you bring me here?"

"Silly Stick, I saw you on the beach and you told me to do so."

"Yes. But why?"

"You tell me, Stick. You're responsible for moving here to live with me. This is my home and you're the guest."

"Humph," responded the Old One.

She didn't talk again for a week. Her head remained turned

into the corner.

After a week of silence, I said, "Alright you, you are a teacher. I know I brought you home because you challenged me on the beach. Made me think on a thing I had in mind to do and stopped it. So I give you your acknowledgment, Old One, willingly. I won't fight you anymore. You are more than a guest. I know this. I'm ready to listen."

The Stick turned her face toward me. She said, "It is good you have always called me an Old One. It is true. I am also your forgottens, here to remind you that alone is not always lonely. I am a root once groundgrown and anchored into the earth. As are you. Always. Listen in yourself to the old parts. They are still good. There is strength in your personal ceremony. It cannot be forgotten for days or left undone. It is your power. I am also water floater. I remind you of that. Water holds up life. Adds to all growing. And, I am a maker of fire. A giver of heat come to remind you that, as I make fire of myself, so do you. You are always in and with yourself. All things are interwoven with others. Nothing can grow or live entirely alone. Enough is said. I am here. You are in you. I am in you."

The Stick stopped speaking. I waited for more but there was none then. She's spoken since. I stop to listen each day now. I touch her in leaving or coming, thanking her for being a friend. Thank the Hall of Grandmothers and the Creator for gifting me sticktalk.

The Saints and Sinners Run

BECKY BIRTHA

*M*y name is Cecily Banks and I drive on the South Street line: Number 40, from Parkside to Society Hill. I work full time—five days a week, and been driving long enough to be off any Saturday or Sunday I want. But the fact is, I rather work on Sunday than any other day. Sunday I don't be worrying about my kids.

Any week day, soon as it get close to three o'clock, I'm starting in to think about them. Wonder if Tammy remembered to wait for Marvin. Hope she didn't lose her key again. Like the last time, when it was pouring down rain, and she was too embarrassed to tell anybody and made Marvin sit on the back step with her so wouldn't no neighbors see they was locked out. I'd been home calling neighbors for half an hour before I figured out where they was.

Wonder if she got any homework—and if she does, I hope she starting to do it, and not gonna wait till I get home, then claim she forgot. I hope they had enough to eat for lunch, and don't eat up the leftovers in there I got planned for tonight's dinner.

Some nights I'd like to call home, just tell Tammy to stick something in the oven. Can't you just see a whole bus fulla people waiting, while I get out at the corner payphone: "Honey, set the dial at three hundred. And open up the icebox door. Now, you see that piece of ham on the second shelf, wrapped up in tin foil? That's right. And down at the bottom there's a bag of string beans...."

It's only a couple of hours from when they get out to when I get off. But those the worst two hours of my day. Schoolkids! Kids today take the prize for being the most impudent, insolent, sassy, brassy, rowdy, rambunctious, and downright fresh of any generation there ever was. We thought we was bad, when we used to get smart with people or answer back. But that little bit of rebellion wasn't nothing, compared to what you see today. And hear.

Friday, a girl wasn't no bigger than my Tammy tried to get on at the front door with a big old cone in her hand, piled way up high with soft custard. I say, "Miss—" I always start out treating them respectful, for all the good it does—"Miss, you can't bring that on the bus." I point to the sign up front, where it very clearly say "No Eating. No Drinking." Of course, I know half these kids can't read, even if they is in junior high, but she can hear me talking to her. She just flash her pass at me and try to march on by. Only the bus is so crowded it ain't exactly easy to slide past, and don't nobody move over to let her by.

"Miss, did you hear me? I said there's no food allowed on this bus."

And she explode. "I ain't deaf. I heard you. But I just spent a M-F-ing dollar on this ice cream cone. How'd I know the M-F-ing bus was gonna come. Don't never come on time no other day. And I got a right to get on this M-F-ing bus. I got a M-F-ing pass."

I say, "Miss, you entitled to your opinion about the bus company regulations. But I just get paid for doing my job. You're gonna have to get off and wait for the next bus."

Lucky for me, she stomps on off the bus. Sometimes it ain't so easy. Sometimes they be slipping them passes from hand to hand so fast you'd think they was doing magic tricks. I've had women's pocketbooks and men's gold chains snatched. I've had to stop everything from break dancing contests to knife fights. Half the time, I'm shaking in my shoes, but I always act real tough. I'll take em on if I have to. I grew up in South Philly myself.

Just this past Friday, way early in the morning, I was pulling off over the South Street bridge when I caught a whiff of smoke. Don't nothing else in the world smell like that — I know it's got to be weed. I can see in my mirror where it must be coming from — a collection of gym bags and long legs in sneakers with the tongues hanging out, sticking way out in the aisle. I turn around. One of em, look like he the ringleader, leaning way back in his seat behind a pair of shades, like this TWA and he cruising at an altitude of 25,000 feet: Mr. Kool himself.

Now I ain't necessarily saying I object to the stuff — in the right place at the right time, with the right company. But the Southeastern Pennsylvania Transportation Authority ain't the right company. "No smoking allowed on the bus." I say it once and it don't make no impression. I say it again, little louder. "There's no smoking allowed on this bus. If you want to smoke, you'll have to get off the bus and do it somewhere else."

We ain't even talking about *what* they smoking. Like I say, I always start out treating em with respect. But some kids don't even know what respect is. So finally I pull on over by the University Stadium, flick on the flashers, and get up and stride all the way to the back of the bus. It gets real quiet. Every kid on the bus got their eyes glued on me, watching to see what I'm fixing to do. Cept of course Mr. Kool & Company — when I get back there they all casually looking out the window, just like they was actually passing some scenery.

Somebody musta put the joint out — ain't nobody even exhaling back here. But I give my rap anyway. "No smoking on the bus. No pipes, cigars, cigarettes, cigarillos, or unidentified illegal substances. Now if you fellas want to smoke you get off the bus. If you want to stay on the bus, you follow the rules." I look around at all of em, but nobody say nothing. So I start back up to the driver's seat. And sure enough, soon as my back is turned, somebody got something to say.

"What's wrong with joint?" some kid sing out. "God made it." And a shot of laughter goes hooting all through the bus.

Now most of the time I just hold my temper and keep my mouth shut, cause I know how hard it is to get the best of these kids. But that time I forgot myself, and I hollered out, just like I was back on my old block down in South Philly, "That's right. God made it. But he didn't plant none on my bus."

The kids all make that noise they make when somebody score one, and I step on the gas and roar off before anybody got time to figure out what the next move gonna be.

Now you can see why I choose to work on Sundays whenever I can. No smartass kids trying to mess with my head. And my own two smartass kids safe at my mama's, and she don't let em mess with *her* head. Sunday mornings on the bus, everything is calm, peaceful, and orderly, just the way I like it. I call it The Saints and Sinners Run—nobody out but the ladies, on the way to church. They flick out their senior citizens' cards and parade on past in their printed silks, white gloves, and little veiled hats, treating me to my own private fashion show.

I pick em up all along Parkside and on through West Philadelphia, and then all the way down South Street, one or two on every corner. Seem like, no matter where people move to, they always want to come back home to their own church, the one they was raised up in. It always gets me thinking about the church I was raised up in myself.

Sunday mornings in the springtime, right around this time of year, the church ladies looked just like a garden. Our little church'd be overflowing with all the pretty colors, just the way those same ladies' little fenced in back yards'd be overflowing with roses and peonies and snowball bushes all summer long. I used to sit there all starched and ironed, and straightened and curled, and listen to the pipe organ starting up with those long, slow notes, and watch the light come slanting in through the colored windows—and I knew why they called that room the sanctuary. There wasn't no question in my mind that that was where God spent his Sunday mornings. God and all the angels, too.

So I like to do that South Street run, because it takes me

130

back. What I like to do is call out the names of the different churches, along with the streets I call out all the other days. Everybody enjoys that. It makes em feel real special, feel recognized — and also kinda lets em know that I respect what they doing, that my working on Sunday don't necessarily mean I don't abide by the ten commandments. Somebody got to ferry people back and forth, so they can worship where they choose on the day they choose. And I see that as my mission.

Once in a while, an old lady will ask me, "Don't you go to church?" She'll be looking up and down my slacks and my man-tailored blue shirt. But that's my uniform. She can see it's pressed clean and fresh on Sunday, just like every other day. And I may have a no nonsense hairdo, but it's neat and trim.

"Yes, ma'am," I say. "When I don't have to work." It's not exactly a lie. The times I go to church *do* be times when I don't have to work. Maybe not *every* time I don't have to work, but she didn't ask that.

"What church you belong to?"

And I say, "North Star Baptist Church." I joined North Star when I was ten years old. I ain't unjoined yet, so I guess I'm still counted among the congregation. And that's always the end of that. She nod her head and smile at me, and go find her a scat on my chariot.

"Twenty-third Street. Gray's Ferry Avenue. Saint Anthony DePadua Chapel." That's an early morning stop, for folks that want to get their church going out of the way. "Church of the Lord Jesus Christ of the Apostle Faith. Apostolic Square." The Apostolic church is a different story. Some of the folks I drop off there'll stay all day. The kids that attend that church is something else — the boys talking in quiet voices, young girls slender, dark and pretty, in their hats and long skirts. They mind their mamas, and their little brothers and sisters mind them. I wish more of their kind would ride on my bus during the week. We still in Saints territory.

"Twenty-second Street. New Central Baptist Church. Twentieth Street. Saint Philip's." Sometimes I think South Philly got the highest concentration of churches in the whole country.

Only thing they got more of is bars. I guess when the church-going folks saw how fast new bars kept opening up, they figured they just had to go on opening up new churches, to try to keep the balance even. "Nineteenth Street. Holy Trinity Baptist. Saint Mary's Episcopal." Every other week I call Saint Mary's first, so the Episcopalians won't think I'm playing favorites. Though I don't suppose they ever lose any sleep worrying over the Baptists, anyway.

"Seventeenth Street. First Colored Wesley Methodist Church, one block to the right. New Light Beulah Baptist Church. Truevine Church of God in Christ." We getting into sinners territory now. It always tickles me how some folks like to go to church feeling holy, and others would rather see themselves as sinners. It must be easier on the sinners — they don't have to put so much into keeping up the image all week long. And the sinners always sound like they having a better time during services, too, making all those joyful noises unto the Lord. Truevine is just a little church, not much more than a storefront, but they got a powerful sound you can hear all the way from South Street.

"Fifteenth Street. Wesley A M E Zion one block to your left, on Lombard Street." And I holler out the names like that, all the way on down through Society Hill. Finally I wind up down past Mother Bethel. Then swing back around to Lombard Street. And that's my run.

This morning start out like any other Sunday. Only thing is, I don't seem to pick up nobody along the way but old ladies. Not even no middle aged ones. Come to think of it, it *was* pretty cloudy this morning when I started out. Only the most faithful servants gonna turn out today, the kind you can identify as churchfolks a block away, even on a weekday.

When I get to Market Street, there's a whole flock of plump, healthy looking sisters in white matron's uniforms, waiting for me. And then the next stop, here comes a woman remind me of my grandma — thin as a twig, in a prim gray dress with little white flowers scattered all over it, and a gold cross around her neck. Hardly five feet tall, with a little blue hat perched up atop her head, and a great big huge straw pocketbook. Next corner, I pick up two or three more. Cloudy days don't bother me none, and I'm feeling pretty good this morning, right on schedule and singing to myself. "Good news, chariot's a coming...."

While I'm waiting for the light to change, I smell something that distinctly smell like fried chicken. And I can hear somebody crumpling those crispy papers all around, getting it out. I take a deep whiff. Mmm-hmm. Hot fried chicken and french fries. I can even smell a little barbecue sauce. I been kinda daydreaming, not paying attention or remembering what day it is. And the next thing I know I'm on my feet, heading for the back of the bus, with my speech already forming in my mind.

Sure enough, somebody got a paper bag opened up, and a paper napkin all spread out in their lap, and their mouth open just getting ready to chomp into a big old piece of fried chicken. Only thing wrong is who it is — that little gray wisp of a woman remind me of my grandma. She looking up at me with that piece of chicken between her fingers, and her feet not even touching the floor. She may be little and skinny and old, but she got a look in her eye make you stop and think twice about what you got to say to her.

"Ma'am," I start out.

"Yes?"

"Uh, ma'am. Excuse me ma'am." I can't seem to get no more words out. Cause the way I was raised up, you don't mess with nobody could be your grandma.

"Yes? What is it?" Kind of voice used to put the fear of God in me.

"Uh, um ..." And then I take a chance and look all around the bus for a second — no, there ain't nobody here cept church go-ers. No kids that ride the bus on weekdays, might remember this. "Well, excuse me, but was you the one wanted to get off at Thirteenth Street?"

She look me right in the eye, like she know I just made that up, and say, "No, I was not."

And I'm backing back to the driver's seat, mumbling "Scuse me, Ma'am. Sorry to trouble you. Just want to make sure

133

nobody don't miss their stop." I step on the gas and holler out, "Twelfth Street. Saint Peter Claver."

I guess the good sister'll finish her fried chicken in her own good time. And I guess she know what stop she want, and she'll manage to get off when she get there. Obviously she don't need no help from me. And I say to myself, "Just drive the bus, Cecily, that's all you gotta do; that's all you getting paid for—just driving the bus. Ain't nobody gonna know what go on on this bus but you and these saints and sinners here, and God. Just stop for the red light. Go when it turn green. Put your wipers on now, it's starting to rain a little bit."

And right that minute I smell it. That thick burnt odor come snaking through the air, all through the bus right up to my driver's seat. It ain't frankincense. Only one thing in the world smell like that—and I don't never allow nobody to smoke it on my bus. Ain't nobody ever tried to before—on Sunday morning!

I got my foot on the brake again, pull back on the hand brake and turn around in my seat. And all there is is gray-haired ladies, wearing crosses and carrying Bibles, with their legs crossed at the ankle and their hands folded in their laps, and the sweetest, most innocent expressions on their faces you ever did see. I look em all over, and everyone of em look me right in the eye. And I shake my head—and turn back around in the driver's seat. Muttering to myself. "Just drive the bus, girl. That's all you getting paid to do."

I don't know which one it was. I don't want to know. Cause even just thinking about somebody's grandma smoking joint on the bus does a job on my head. There's certain things you come to depend on about the way the world supposed to operate. When I see some teenage kid with a twenty pound radio on his shoulder, I know he ain't gonna be reading no Bible on the bus. But this morning the hoodlums and the saved souls all mixed up together in my head. Used to be I could tell em apart. Now I don't know what to expect. I can still smell that distinct aroma, hanging in the air, all the way down to Mother Bethel.

When I get to the end of the run, I park the bus and shut off the motor to take my break. And then go cross the street to a telephone booth, and do something I ain't hardly ever done, all the years I been working for the Transportation Authority. I dial my mama's number.

"Hi, Ma. Cecily here."

"What happened, honey? What's wrong? You have an accident? You all right?"

I'm feeling kinda silly already, and not exactly sure why I did call. "No, nothing's wrong. I just got to thinking about the kids ... and you, wondering if ... everything's okay."

"Now you know better than that." I can hear her voice get all huffy, the way it does when she's insulted. "You know you don't need to worry about Tammy and Marvin when they're with me. You oughtta save your quarters for something you might need em for."

"Yeah, I guess you right. I just thought I'd see how you all was getting along today. Uh ... how's Grandma doing ?" My grandma just moved in with my mother a couple months ago.

"She's fine. I'm fine. The kids fine. Everybody doing just fine. You better go get yourself something to eat, before your break is up."

"Yeah, I am." Don't seem like much left for me to say. "Uh, would you put Tammy on the line a second?"

Seem like she get real quiet all of a sudden.

"Tammy's not here right now."

"Not there?" What I feel like is like somebody come up and laid a nice friendly hand on my back—and then clobbered me over the head. "Not there?"

"Now just calm down. She's not here because she went to church. Her and Marvin both went."

"They went to church?" It don't sound too likely. Church ain't never been Tammy's favorite place to be on a Sunday morning. Marvin's neither.

"They didn't go by themselves. They went with Grandma. Out to Fifty-ninth Street."

"Fifty-ninth Street?" Nothing is making any sense.

"Yes. You know. To her old church. Fifty-ninth Street Baptist Church. And Cecily, it ain't gonna harm those two none to get a little Christian training now and then. It ain't gonna hurt em at all."

I can't think what to say. I oughtta feel reassured. But I'm still feeling clobbered. Like things ain't in my own hands any more.

"Look," she says. "You know Tammy and Marvin just as safe with us as when they with you. You know Grandma wouldn't let nothing happen to her babies. So just set your mind at rest."

After I hang up the phone, I wander back cross the street and climb on up in the driver's seat. She's right. Shouldn't be nothing wrong with a nice old lady taking her two great grandkids to church on Sunday morning. I turn on the lights, start up the motor, open the doors. But my mind is not at rest. I keep thinking about Tammy, Marvin, Grandma ... the schoolkids and the church ladies, like they all part of a puzzle I can't figure out — don't know where to start. Wonder what *do* go on in all these churches. I always thought I knew.

When I zip past Thirty-eighth Street, somebody's grandma is tapping me on the shoulder, saying, "Excuse me, Miss, but isn't this bus supposed to turn on Thirty-eighth?"

And it's a good thing she did it, too. I'd a been clear out to the Fifty-ninth Street Baptist Church by now.

The Plasting Project

MERLIN STONE

*A*s she walked down the hallway of the Time Consciousness Building, Telore could hear voices coming from the Plasting Room. She was relieved to hear that Roweta was there, a fact made clear by Roweta's soft musical tones chiming along with a few others. But a small frown formed on Telore's brow. She had hoped to be able to speak with Roweta privately. Perhaps she should wait until that evening when they would be having dinner at home. After all, Telore's decision to transfer to an office so far away and to break up her longstanding relationship with Roweta was no minor matter. But she couldn't wait. The news was too pressing, too urgent to keep to herself.

As Telore approached the doorway of the large, brightly lit room, she saw Fanille and Andorah both sitting on the blue lounge, their young legs sprawled out at odd angles. The familiar models of ancient temples sat on the table near the wall that was covered with drawings of archaic statues and artifacts. Roweta was leaning forward in the armchair at her desk by the broad window, engrossed in the conversation, the varied greens beyond the window haloing her delicate face, highlighting the pale jade hue of her eyes.

"I think it's time we inserted the new tablets somewhere in Paraguay," Andorah was insisting.

"I know you want to get on with that project, Andorah,"

replied Roweta gently, "but the Time Consciousness Council feels that they are not nearly ready yet. They haven't even found the buried library we placed in Zimbabwe."

"I just knew we were setting it too deep," murmured Fanille almost to herself.

Roweta spun around at her desk and pressed a few keys on the Time Consciousness Board. She leaned back in her armchair as they watched the wall screen above the desk. The familiar rotating globe began to appear. It was marked with five tiny red lights.

"See," Roweta was saying as though the discussion was settled, "there are still five of our plastings lying there undiscovered by them. I was wondering if all that fighting to the east of the Mediterranean Sea might at least uncover those tablets we left near Beirut but they are all so blinded by their claims about who owns what and their need to 'get even,' as they say, they're probably tripping over those tablets without even noticing them."

"She's right, Andorah," Fanille conceded softly, "there's no sense in our going any further with new plastings until they catch up with what we've already done."

Telore stood in the doorway, her tall thin form unobserved and silent. As one of the oldest members of the Time Consciousness Department she realized immediately that this conversation reflected the usual impatience with the Earth Beings, the ones who called themselves humans, the one species in the Universe that seemed to refuse to develop. From the day the Time Consciousness Department had begun the project of planting the past on Earth, plasting as they called it, they had met with little success. One of the first problems that TCD had encountered was that the lighter beings, some of the ones who referred to themselves as Caucasians, had begun to think that they were in charge of the entire planet and everything and everyone else on it. In an effort to correct that situation the TCD had planted the ruins of Sumer in Iraq and those of Harappa in India, to show the lighter ones that the darker beings had developed as inventive and literate humans even before they did. But a few of the lighter ones just muddled the evidence and then announced that it had been their own ancestors who were responsible for those early developments. Of all the plastings the TCD had done, in China, in Africa, in Mexico — nothing had really worked to solve the problem.

Trying to decide if she should return later, when Roweta was alone, Telore found herself thinking of the day the Plasting Project had been officially launched, when she and Roweta had been elected by the TCD Council as co-directors of the project. They had so hoped that when the beings of Earth began to think about a very long past, it would help them to conceive of a very long future ahead. The ultimate goal of the project was to help Earth Beings to understand why it was so important for them to protect and preserve the natural resources of their planet for that future. Yet from the day that the initial work of the Plasting Project had begun, the air and waters of Earth, the very ground, had become even more polluted, even more poisoned.

"Well, maybe the whole idea just won't work," Andorah was saying. "They're so stupid. Have you noticed that every time we plast a female jaw bone or a female cranium, to help them understand that there were mostly females in the beginning of their species, they call it Swanscombe Man or Peking Man? I'm beginning to think that this whole experiment should be scrapped. They're just not getting any of the information or perceptions we've been trying to communicate."

"Still, we must keep trying," replied Roweta, with the calm of her 9000 years. "It's true that they are slower and less developed than we expected when we began but it's not an impossible task. After all, it's only been about 200 days since we started this operation — what they would count as 200 years on Earth. Before that many of the beings of Earth had a completely distorted idea about when and how they got there. Some nonsense about being made in seven days! At least some of them have now begun to think about the chronological enormity of their own development."

"That's true," commented Telore, unable to stay out of the

conversation any longer. Roweta looked up and smiled in pleasant surprise as Telore entered the room. "And the materials we recently planted about The Mother of the Universe are catching on like a forest fire in a high wind. It seems that many of the females on Earth are studying the materials that we left there. Remember those little symbolic statues of The Mother that we scattered all over the place on one of our first plasting missions? Well, according to the reports we're receiving they are becoming quite popular among the females. Moreover, many of them really are beginning to think about the past, and even the future, in a totally different way. Maybe our problem has been in trying to communicate with just anyone there. It was invariably the males who kept searching for most of the materials we plasted and they were interpreting and deciding what they were—all too often, incorrectly. The females do seem to be more open, more able to grasp our messages."

Roweta motioned to Telore to sit in the chair beside her but Telore shook her head and remained standing near the doorway, obviously nervous and attentive.

"Telore's right," said Andorah quickly, trying to ease the tension in Telore, though she had no idea what might be causing it. "If all the females, or at least a lot of them, lived in one area it would make our job so much easier. It shouldn't be this difficult. All we're really trying to do is to get the Earth Beings to stop competing with each other long enough to understand that they're living on one of the most richly endowed and beautiful planets in the entire universe. Why, it's almost as ideal as our own. If only they would stop poisoning it and destroying it."

"You know," said Telore, "the Time Consciousness Council was certain that if we could help the Earth Beings to develop a broader and deeper consciousness of time, of past and future, that's exactly what would happen. And the idea does make sense. For one thing, once they realized that they developed from one common ancestral stock, they might be able to see themselves as members of the same family and be able to cooperate with each other."

Telore turned toward Roweta with a faintly nostalgic smile.

"Do you remember when the Earth Being known as Darwin made them think about longer expanses of time and process and we were so excited? We really thought that once they understood there was such a thing as a very ancient past behind them, they would begin to be able to conceive of a very long future ahead. We were so sure that a natural desire to cooperate in protecting their planet for that future would develop in them at that time. But they thought that 'survival of the fittest' meant conquering or killing others and did not realize it had more to do with the wisdom of learning to adapt and to live in tune with nature. And then again, when they finally found the materials we plasted at Olduvai Gorge, our expectations were so high. But nothing really changed."

She paused for a moment as her voice softened with a note of sorrow. "It's so painful to get our hopes up each time just to have them crushed over and over again." Roweta nodded in sad agreement.

Fanille stood up and walked over to the large window, staring out as though her thoughts were far removed from the Plasting Room. The youthfulness of her 1800 years made her somewhat hesitant about expressing her own insights, especially to older Council members such as Telore and Roweta. She suddenly turned back to the others in the room as the intensity of her thoughts forced her to speak them aloud.

"It seems very obvious that the females would be the ones to understand our messages more easily. Their own biological time cycles would naturally make them more capable of comprehending our concepts. And from what I've read, it's the females who are most often able to hear the murmurings of the oceans and trees and mountains and the voices of the other animals on Earth. I'm surprised that no one thought of that at the start of this project."

"We knew so much less about Earth Beings when we began," Telore explained. "We have been talking at the Council meetings about how much energy we've already spent on this Earth project and searching for new ways to speed up the process." Telore paused for a long moment, as if deciding whether or not

141

to say something and then added, "Especially now, because the Council thinks that it's time to let them know about what happened to the planet Hephaistos."

Although they were clearly surprised by this unexpected announcement, Fanille and Andorah both nodded their heads in immediate agreement.

"The big question we have," continued Telore, "as always, is how best to let them know. If we just plast another piece of evidence, or even a lot of evidence, it might be too late before they discover it. And even if they find it somewhat more quickly than they generally do, there would probably be the usual long drawn-out arguments about what it indicated and whether or not it was authentic."

Andorah's voice rang with impatience. "But once the beings of Earth realize that the ring of asteroids between what they call Mars and Jupiter are the remains of Hephaistos—the horrible reminders of that day when the Hephaistian governments of Usar and Rusar made a small error in their computations and blew their whole planet to shreds and splinters—surely that knowledge would bring the Earth Beings to their senses."

"Some of them do know something about it," said Roweta thoughtfully, "although they talk about it as Atlantis or Lemuria and think of it as an island in one of their Earth seas. Most of the others regard the memory of what happened as total fantasy, yet it does linger on in their legends."

"We've been discussing this Earth problem with Time Consciousness offices everywhere," explained Telore, "trying to devise the very best methods of letting the Earth Beings know what happened to the planet of Hephaistos in a way they will believe—and as quickly as possible. One of the most ironic and discouraging aspects of this whole project is that the few Hephaistians who escaped from their planet before it exploded fled to Earth and settled there among the indigenous Earth Beings. And those Hephaistians were the very ones who were primarily responsible for that unforgettable disaster. No one else had access to the spaceships they used to get off the planet in time to survive. From what we can tell, some of the Earth

Beings of today may have inherited the DNA of those few Hephaistians who made it to Earth at that time. They seem to be the ones who now want to build stations and colonies in space, all the while piling up nuclear explosives and wastes on Earth. It's as if they have some genetic memory that allows them to think that they will be able to escape from Earth if a time comes when it is necessary to do so."

"Well, I sure hope they don't come here," remarked Andorah.

A heavy silence pervaded the room, each of them slipping deep into her own thoughts for several long moments. Roweta tried to engage Telore's attention but Telore seemed to be completely absorbed in examining the model of an ancient building.

"The females!" Fanille shouted, shattering the silence. "We've got to reach the females! It's our only chance. It's their only chance. I mean for *all* of the Earth Beings — and all those other dear creatures that live there with the humans. They do have such sweet animals on Earth. Did you see the kitten I brought back from our last mission?"

Roweta's face brightened. "I suppose we did not seriously consider that, did we Telore? At the time we initiated the Plasting Project 200 days ago, no one on Earth ever listened to what the females said. But just very recently the females have made it possible to announce their discoveries publicly, even to interpret and explain them to the others. Of course, the males do still make it difficult for them to do that but the females seem to have made a lot of headway in this area. Before Fanille said that, I had just been thinking that the plasting of the Hephaistos material would have to be so specific, so obvious, that even the most arrogant and stubborn of the males would have to believe it — and take it seriously. But Fanille is right. We've got to try to reach the females directly."

"I think I've got it!" announced Fanille with an almost visibly expanding sense of self assurance and clarity caused by Roweta's positive response to her suggestion. "We could construct a full scale copy of one of the spaceships that were used by the escaping government officials of Hephaistos, perfect in every detail, and place a daily log inside the cabin, a log that recorded exactly how and why Hephaistos was destroyed."

"That's a great idea!" said Andorah, her mood of pessimism changing to one of excitement. "But where could we plast it so that they would find it quickly enough? The situation is pretty bad there on Earth. It's incredibly like those days before the end of Hephaistos. There may not be much more time."

"We'd have to set it quite close to the surface so they would find it right away," Roweta thought aloud, more excited and hopeful than she had been for a long time. "And in a place where they would not realize it hadn't been before. And the log should be in a language they could decipher quickly and easily. Maybe pictographs — they're pretty obvious."

"This could be just the idea we've been looking for," said Telore. "It's certainly worth discussing further in the Council. And thanks to what Fanille and Andorah have been saying, I just had an idea about the location of the plasting. I've heard reports of a group of females who have formed a peace encampment in a place they call New York State. From what I hear, they appear to have grasped at least a good part of our message already. Perhaps we could plast an Hephaistian spaceship near where that group might be likely to dig for gardens or for wells. And, now that I'm thinking about plasting locations, there's another group of females who have formed a peace camp at a site known as Greenham Common. That's on the other side of that great sea they speak of as the Atlantic. Fanille, Andorah, would you do a thorough geo check on both of those areas in the archives?"

As Fanille and Andorah disappeared down the hall, almost running in their excitement, Telore finally found herself alone with Roweta. She had been needing this chance to be alone with her since she arrived in the middle of the discussion they were having. But now, Telore's plan to transfer to another office, to leave Roweta, suddenly seemed wrong, pointless. They had spent so many wonderful years together, sharing both the joys and sorrow of their lives. And if Telore was hungry for new adventures, as she had felt just that morning, this plan to plast Hephaistian spaceships on Earth, this new idea of how to make Earth Beings really understand the possible consequences of their destructive activities, was as much of a challenge as any she could imagine. Perhaps they really could save Earth, a dream they had shared for such a long time.

She took Roweta's hand in her own. "Roweta, tomorrow morning when we talk to the Council about building the rockets to plast on Earth, let's suggest that Fanille and Andorah do the one at Greenham. It's up to them, of course. But, now don't laugh at me," Telore paused with an unusually shy hesitancy, "I know we're getting older but let's volunteer for the plasting in New York State. We haven't been away together in a long time. We might even enjoy spending some time with the female beings at the peace encampment. I've heard they welcome older females. Do you think they'll believe us when we tell them we've been together for over 3000 years?"

Why The Moon Is Small and Dark When The Sun Is Big and Shiny

A Midrash for Rosh Chodesh*

JUDITH STEIN

*I*n the beginning of the world, the sun and the moon were created as two great lights in the sky. But the moon was jealous of the sun, and wanted to be the only light. One story says that She Who Created the Worlds was so angered by the moon's jealousy that She took away the moon's light. The moon would be smaller, with no light of her own, lit only by the reflection of the sun when their paths crossed. This would be the moon's punishment for jealousy.

Now that is what we are told when we ask why the moon is small and dark, but what we are told is often not the same as what is true. The moon would no more be jealous of the sun than an oyster would be of an elm tree. Each is simply different

---

*Midrash: a teaching legend, designed to provoke thought, to provide an answer by providing a question.
Rosh Chodesh: literally, head of the month; a celebration of the new moon.

from the other, each with her own work in the weaving of creation.

But now it's Rosh Chodesh, and we welcome the moon back into her growing cycle, and you want to know: why is the moon so small and dark when the sun is big and shiny? Nu, I'll tell you what I think is the true story, who's to know for sure?

It is true that the moon and the sun started out as two great lights circling in the sky. They did discuss their light, and maybe the discussions became a little heated or loud. But there was never any jealousy or animosity between the moon and the sun. It was simply that they travelled along the same path, since the beginning of time, and they had a lot to say to each other. You know how it can be, with two old friends who have discussed everything a million times and still have lots of time to fill. No matter how much they love each other, they also love nothing better than to have a good argument.

Meanwhile, the moon and the sun are circling, circling, always together, and to tell you the truth, maybe they are just a little bored. As they circle they stir up dust, and the dust begins to form something solid — a little planet, our planet — the Earth. Or, if you prefer, knowing they were bored and had millenia to travel, She Who Created the Worlds created our earth to give them something to talk about.

However it happened, our little home emerged, and the sun and moon began to discuss our planet. They would comment on the creation of the oceans and the land, the mountains and the huge forests. A few million circles later, they noticed other forms of life on what had been a pile of nothingness not so long before. They delighted in telling each other tales of what they saw as they passed the earth. It was a pleasure to have this new planet to talk about. Each of them wanted to get a better view of what was happening there. It was so hard to see from so far away, and by now clouds had been formed which got in the way.

On one trip, the sun decided to move in closer to the earth. Not much closer, you understand, but enough to begin a burning heat in the air, so hot that the earth below became parched and dry. The forests turned to ash, the waters dried up, and the dark rich earth became a tawny golden color. As soon as the sun saw what had happened, she pulled herself back. But it was too late. That part of the earth was never again to regain the wet lushness it lost; it remained forever dry and golden, with little water. For several million cycles the sun was so full of despair and remorse that there was no consoling her, and she would barely speak to her beloved friend as they travelled together.

The moon tried to persuade the sun to look at that burned part of the earth as she passed. The sun usually grew silent and stared into space, unwilling to see again the damage she had caused. But the moon kept talking about new life, and changes, so the sun gathered her courage and then, as they passed the barren spot, looked down.

What she saw shocked her so much that she wobbled on her path! That barren wasteland was gone, replaced by something living — dry, but definitely alive. There were a few trees, of a new tougher-looking kind. There were patches of water here and there, and there were animals. The sun was so thrilled at what she saw she sang a song of exaltation. The moon caught her mood, and together they sang a haunting melody for many cycles.

Then, for a while, it was like old times. The sun and moon would talk and discuss and argue about all they had seen, how such a burning waste could become such fertile ground. They began to feel that this spot of the earth was special; that it had almost died, but instead revived, full of new life. The sun and moon became curious, about what would happen next. How would the creatures below live? How would they spend their time? Would they learn the pleasure of loving arguments?

But after another million turns, the sun and moon had nothing new to say. What they could see from so far away was so little and faint. Both of them knew how deadly it would be to get closer, but they felt so drawn to the earth and the creatures below. They dreamed of ways to get closer as they circled in silence.

One day the moon announced that she had a plan. She was the smaller of the two, she said. Not only was she smaller, but her capacity to carry light was smaller. Since she was too small to carry the sun's light, the moon would give her own light to the sun to carry until she might want it again. Then she would be dark and cool, and could go very close to the earth, and listen and watch, but do no harm to the creatures living there.

The sun laughed with delight at the moon's plan, until she realized that they would no longer be companions as they had been for all time. The moon might find out everything about the earth: the kinds of trees upon it, and the animal creatures of every kind, but the knowledge would remain silent with her on her lonely small path around the earth. Then both of them grew sad because they knew that knowledge without companionship is a cold, barren comfort. It seemed they were faced with two terrible choices: to travel together with no chance of new knowledge, or to travel with learning but always alone. Both the sun and moon became morose, and they circled silently many times.

Very much later, the moon spoke. She said "Beloved friend, I may have a solution. I don't know where the idea came from..." Now some say that She Who Created the Worlds grew filled with compassion for the sun and the moon, and planted the idea in the moon's dreams. Who's to say? Wherever it came from, this was the moon's idea. She would give her light to the sun to carry, and set out on a new and smaller circle around the earth. The sun would continue on almost the same path, but it would become a bit more oval. These new paths would cross once in every one of the moon's cycles. Each cycle they would be together again, for a very short time.

The sun smiled as she realized what a good plan this was, and said a silent thank you to She Who Created the Worlds for having helped them in their dilemma. The sun knew they would lose their constant companionship, but they would get closer to the earth and the creatures below. And when they met each cycle, they could talk, they could discuss, maybe they could even argue. It seemed like a very good plan.

The sun and moon discussed this plan for many cycles, tossing the idea, and turning it, and sometimes simply moving together in silence as they contemplated separating from each other. Around and around they moved, sailing through their indecision until finally, they turned and looked lovingly at each other.

The sun said "My friend, my beloved moon, I will miss your constancy more than I can say. I'll long for our time together. I'll treasure the time I have alone to think about what you tell me. And I'll hope that our time together is a time to talk, to discuss, maybe even have a little argument."

As the moon's great round eyes filled with tears, she turned to her beloved friend and said: "I give you my light and warmth to hold for me in safekeeping. I'll learn what I can about the earth and the creatures upon her. I'll tell them about us, how we travelled together from the beginning of time. I'll ask them to honor our cycles together, and our paths when we part. And I'll show them our beauty, through your reflection on me. Through me they'll know both of us."

With these last words, the moon began a great wrenching change in her path. She tore herself away from the sun, sometimes feeling as though she were tearing herself in two. As she moved further away, she took her light and her heat and tossed them through the sky to her beloved companion. As the sun caught it, the light grew so bright that the moon was in awe. "We are beautiful together," she thought, as her path took her further away.

As the moon began her cycle around the earth, she began to shine with the light reflected from the sun. She sang to earth; a song which told how the sun and moon had travelled together for so long, but had become lonely with only each other. She sang of how she longed for the time in her cycle when she and the sun were together again. It might look like she were darkened and gone, but she would return. Without ceasing, the moon sang her love song to earth. She only paused during that brief moment when she and the sun travelled together.

Now, you might ask, how much did the creatures below understand of her song? Well, the moon never knew, and I couldn't say. Each month we pay homage to the path of the moon as she waxes and wanes, and finally grows dark. At Rosh Chodesh we welcome her light as she returns once again to us. Now, when we see her again, we might listen more closely for her sweet refrain.

The old stories may tell us of jealousy and punishment if we ask why the moon has no light of her own. But maybe it's from the love of the moon for the sun, and their love of a good argument. Which story is right? Who could say for sure?

Ernesta

JUDY GRAHN

*R*eversing *a perilous situation doesn't necessarily mean skinning the cat*

Five brown young girls moved down by the riverside, stirring the bushes with the motions of their bodies. They ranged in age from the eldest to the youngest and they spoke quietly, disturbing little around them, for it was late in the day and they were tired. They were not all together very often, but on this particular evening they were all together and they acted completely as a unit.

They were late for home without having done what they had been sent out for, and they knew it. Their chore was to each pull up a bundle of reeds or wickers growing in the shallow water close to the bank. The reeds were to be dried and dyed and used to make mats and trays for the midsummer festival only two weeks away. The eldest moved the fastest, frantic to collect the hard stubborn plants along the river. The reeds had been admirable and friendly in the morning but now had turned into deep-rooted enemies who surrendered to their tugging with ill-will. She knew they were being rude and hasty, so that the plants bit them.

"Come-up, come-up," the eldest whispered desperately as she yanked on them, and her hands began blistering however she couldn't stop before they had gathered each a good load, because she knew that the youngest child, who was very literal about directions, would not give up until they had gotten the proper quota of reeds.

In a few minutes the earth had turned away from the sun, and they were doing their work in near darkness. When she thought they would all agree with her, the eldest said, "That's enough," and they started for home.

Nobody had complained, though she thought she heard somebody's nose running, probably from the pain of the blisters; her own hands stung from the fury of biting plants, but she forgot them as they quickly pulled themselves up the slippery bank and found the narrow trail after a few false fumblings in the underbrushes.

They walked swiftly in long-legged strides, single-file, only a few yards down a trail which was exactly as wide as they were, and then the eldest stopped dead short and all the others ran into the one ahead.

Facing them on the trail, and on her way down to the river for a drink of water, was a mother lion. She stopped too, and there they stood for the longest time, all examining each other with big eyes. The lion smelled them and knew they were from the town two miles west of where they were now, that they were frightened above eveything else, and that they had been in the water; she also knew they would taste very good if she put her mind in *that* direction, and she did, because she nearly always did, that being her occupation.

They smelled her and knew that she had kittens somewhere, since she had a milky odor under the dusty lion smell. More than that they couldn't tell.

The eldest and first in line kept her eyes on the lion's eyes and mentally rehearsed everything she had ever heard about the lion family; because in split seconds she would have to make the decision of what-to-do-next.

It occurred to one of them that this might be the lion who had eaten her uncle's favorite goat last year, but she couldn't afford to be mad about it at the moment. The oldest and first in line tried to spread her vision to see if she could make out the out-lines of kittens behind their mother, and could not. They must be very little, and home in bed. She tried to smell if the lion had eaten recently, but could detect no bloodsmell.

The eldest knew that their only weapon was a knife, and she was not carrying it, and couldn't remember who was; a mistake she would never make again. Then she remembered what was important about today, that it was the hottest day anyone could remember since last summer; a day so blistery that they could not resist swimming it away; and that meant the countryside was dry; and that meant the mother lion was probably more thirsty right now than she was hungry.

Having decided on a solution, she took a breath and dropped one hand slowly from her bundle of reeds, and reaching behind herself, she pushed the leg of the next girl backwards, as a signal. Then the next dropped her hand from her bundle of reeds and pushed back on the next and the next on the next un-til the youngest child got the signal and took one giant step backwards; then they all took one giant step backwards while at the same moment the lion took one giant step forwards. In this manner, and with none of them making a sound except when their feet touched the ground, they all backward walked to the river until the youngest child stood on the bank and took one more happy step and fell into the river. The eldest, still with her eyes staring at the yellow eyes, knew when she heard the splash that she only had four more steps to go, and sure enough, soon they were all in the water, reeds clutched every which way, frantically swimming downstream. The one who could not swim pulled herself along with vines and roots hang-ing from the marshy bank. The mother lion watched them go with no comment, sniffed the air, walked to a low place in the bank, and drank enough water to drown anyone.

In the clutches of three large aunts

In a city of dreamers the women say they dream babies into their bellies from spirits and the men dream of hunting animals who no longer live around the vicinity.

Off the street within the walls of a small workyard of the Snake clan, the clan of healing and balancing, a female child is neatly unobtrusively playing. Her clan baby cousins lie sleeping for the afternoon in houses behind her. Her elder cousins are all grown up and gone to work as shepherds. She herself has dark brown skin and kinky black hair near her head, a sturdy body with a slightly round stomach and large hands. She has one eye set straight in her head, the other eye wandering off to the left. She is squatting and arranging ceaselessly a wide variation of small bottles and jars on the ground in front of her, and is mumbling to herself; and is very serious and is called: *Ernesta.*

She had turned her head to the right to listen to a donkey arguing with someone in the distance but when she is called: *Ernesta,* she turns her head to the left, so that her eye wanders up even more, seeming to be staring straight at the sky; and anyone looking is tempted somewhat to laugh but controlling it, then seeing the rest of her face, the solid-featured heaviness of it, anyone puts away their laugh and takes the eye more seriously than they would if it did not have a wandering eye, which is a form of justice.

"Mama?" Ernesta asks, although the caller steps out of the shaded doorway and is not exactly her mama being rather her aunt, Aunt One, whereupon the eye wanders more and is huge.

Aunt One knows that Ernesta was first in a line of girls from various clans who recently escaped a perilous situation with a mama lion who had nearly undone them.

Knowing this lengthens her square face of concern. She says, "What are you doing out here?"

"Oh, I'm just waiting for something to happen," Ernesta says. Actually she has been remembering five girls walking in a line three days before; she has been lining up the pots and jars on the ground before her naming them, "First there was me, then Jessi-ma from the Bee clan, then Fran-keen from the Lion clan. Next was Dee. No, next was Margedda who is such a weird person and then Dee was last from the Barley people." This was helping her remember who was who and how it had all gone that day when everything changed.

Aunt One moves with a soft-footed marching motion, she wears a long dull red dress of filmy material of her own making with pins holding it together at the shoulder. Her niece wears a faded red skirt with no top and very little bottom. Aunt One's hands are full of dried plant fibers, yellow and tan which she calls her wickers.

"Waiting will not cause something to happen," she says sharply. "Nor prevent it either."

She crosses the courtyard to a place with a bowl of water where she sloshes her wickers. Aunt One is making a basket; she sings while she does this.

Aunt One often sings. Everyone sings for many reasons; Aunt One often sings for her own amusement. She sings to remind herself what she is doing. She sings to placate the spirits of boredom. Today Aunt One's song is about a crane who stood for so long in one place on one leg that she hardened into that position, and was unable to lay eggs or get about at all until a supple green snake came along who she persuaded to stiffen itself and be her second leg, whereafter she could walk with not so much trouble although everyone made fun of her and called her a green legged crane.

The entirety of Ernesta's clan, the Snake clan, is happy these days; everything is in harmony with their ways, nothing is in dissension with them. By midsummer's eve their own major clan workyard will have a complicated tile mural picturing some of their more important stories. These included a story of Aunt One and her three sisters importing acacia trees in a procession carrying the tree bundles from the sea side dock and transplanting them into one of their medicine gardens. Soon the story of the procession would be part of a brilliantly colored mural, glazed and shiny with a permanent record of Snake clan power, the power of certain people to effect transformations on living matter.

Aunt One and two of her sisters had brought the mural matter up with the council of elders recently wrangling it through with no problems except a slight argumentation from the Bee clan. The wonderful story tiles would be baked by the Bee clan as was proper and then set into place in the wall of the major workyard by the time for the midsummer festival.

The tail end of Aunt One's basketmaking song includes this current information which she sings loudly as she weaves her wickers. The more recent version of her song has forty two verses taking the better portion of one hour to sing and she enjoys every one of them.

Ernesta does not hear the end of the long song. Her attention has returned to her rows of little baskets and jars, miniatures of the ones used by adults, made long ago when she was a small child, each one a child's size with a child's contents of dust or selected pebbles or barley meal leftover from the cooking larder.

She has made variations of the mixtures, and the discovery that water mixed with dirt and grain and left in the sun for a week or so renders a baked mass that will neither go in nor out of any jar, and is ugly looking besides. Information so useful it never needs to be remembered again yet having something to do with learning the nature of cooking. Memory is important to Ernesta and so is cooking. In Ernesta's clan, cooking and the making of chemical mixtures are one and the same thing.

How cooking took a long time to learn

Ernesta knows that cooking took a long time to learn because she herself is a primary example. Ordinarily many people do the cooking together but one time left to her own devices in the kitchen, she had put honey in the vegetables and salt in the fruit. She had boiled the milk and left the bread dough nearly raw, just lukewarm. Her relatives had threatened to make her eat the whole composition by herself, all of it, to better appreciate her own creativity.

"I didn't burn anything," she protested. They were not impressed by this.

Ernesta's family have a thorough understanding of how cooking took a long time to learn, because they invented it, or so they say; the entire hundred thousand year long process is analoged in their songs with many variations including the difficulty of combining fire with water.

When Ernesta had put salt in the fruit her mother had said, "Ernesta has imagination."

"Not so," Aunt Two said, "that's not imagination. She just doesn't pay attention when she is taught. Ernesta has no memory, therefore she makes things up as she goes along."

Ernesta worried about this a great deal, for in her family a good memory was an imperative. She worked on her memory, reciting avidly when no one was looking: salt for vegetables and curing; salt for cheese but not for teas; honey for bread and open wounds, honey for milk only in the morning or when someone has a stomach ache; onions and garlic for nearly anything though not for melons. She worked on her memory when she was very young and anxious until it became a habit with her mumbling to herself the litany of whatever she might be in danger of forgetting. This habit gave her an excellent memory which her doubting aunts tested her on considerably.

"Smell this," Aunt Three would say, holding a little jar of crushed petals under Ernesta's nose. "What is it called? What foods is it used in and what medicines? How much do you use, where does it come from? If you boiled it with cloth, what color would come out?"

"Feel this powder, Ernesta," Aunt Two would say. "What liquids does it mix with? What did I tell you about it yesterday, where does it come from?"

It remained a puzzle to her for some time about cooking why some things are never eaten raw, like barley; and some are never cooked, like lettuce. Beer appeared only at festivals, berries only in the early summer. Why don't you put butter on *everything,* for instance oranges; why can't you ever put onions in the apple cider. Why are there a hundred ways to eat squash but only a few ways to eat melons when in the fields the squashes and melons look almost the same. These things are peculiar about cooking; these and thousands of other details Ernesta had to learn concerning mixtures which took a long time in the beginning as well as presently.

In the meantime she lined up her jars, a thin one for Jessima, a heavy one for Margedda, a short one for Dee. She was not so much playing since she had actually outgrown this sort of toy as she was trying to puzzle out a thought. She put in place in the little line an unpainted jar to stand for Fran-keen and then a most interesting and decorated elder one first in the line, for herself. Then she reconstructed her memory. Here they were walking up the trail from the river where they pulled themselves out soaking wet. She scratched a long slender mark beside the line of jars for the trail; she scratched other marks off to the right where the new canals were being built by the Bee clan; and then farther to the right she made a wide scratch for the riverroad, where everyone knew a dead woman had been found that same afternoon, three days before. She laid a short woman-representing stick on the spot with reverence.

An enclosed space in a city with light and air is for young children; in this city the walls of every four ground-floor rooms form courtyards of many sizes. These are often with trees or shrubs for shade and company; more often they are with gardens and henyards. There are four clans in the city altogether; the yards of this particular one are lined with pots and plots of herbs and nursling plants. Ernesta's clan being the healing people always smelled of sharp powders and spices they used in their processes. All her babyhood she had played with old or imitation powders and had been warned sharply away from the places in the area where the Aunts kept their more volatile drugs. Fear that their babies would eat the leaves of powerful plants had caused the women of Ernesta's clan to build a large formal temple with a plant nursery on the second floor, guarded by heavy doors that could not be pushed open by little fingers easily.

The four clans altogether are:
The Snake clan, of transformation, healing and mixtures.
The Bee clan, of constructions and water bearing women, and

the keeping of measurements.

The Lion clan, of animals, transportation and trading.

The Tortoise or Barley clan, of farming, provision, distribution of necessities and the keeping of records.

In a city of dreamers the people are held together by a mutual knowing of a strong natural power whose name they call: *Ana* and who is a lady of many faces, some other names and a great deal of body.

Handiwork is just another name for manual labor

Anyone who makes baskets all day long for several days will get blisters, but not Aunt One. Aunt One has hardly callused hands and is an expert. The thin green branch of a willow tree wound around in a circle and woven together with itself by skinny water-soaked strips of long sharp wicker leaves will eventually form a sturdy basket but anyone who makes baskets all day long will get blistered. Except Aunt One, who is however annoyed at the amount of work it takes to make a good midsummer festival. She has sworn not to make any more containers though everyone knows she will anyway because her two younger sisters can always think of more things to put in them. Aunt One wonders if it is wise to have sisters with so much imagination.

Aunt One has been working on the same basket for six months; it is now so tall that only the black top of her hair shows as she stands inside of it, working. She hums a song to help herself along and also to breathe a good spirit into the container. She wants nothing to ever rot secretly at the bottom of it, she wants nothing to ever leak out of its sides. She has incorporated a pattern of red and black into the walls, intermittently a long wavey snake figure and a crane with red body and black legs and head; there are nine of these figures all the way around. The head of each crane is as large as the palm of Aunt One's hand. They stand for transformations of the spirit, something which their designer is hoping for herself, who has been depressed lately on account of arthritis in her hands, and is dreading the chill of winter.

Even a Snake clan woman of transformations can be in need of transformations. Ernesta does not know that her first aunt is depressed by what is happening to her hands; she believes that Aunt One's new gnarley knuckles and oddly bending fingers are an invention of her person, Aunt One's creation of a variation in her own form. She is amazed by this, for she herself even practicing cannot get her hands into such positions; it seems to her a further proof of Aunt One's complete control over her own physical matters.

Ernesta fixed her wandering eye on Aunt One's head, barely showing. Aunt One had told her that meeting a lion on the trail was the reversing of a perilous situation, and from then on that was how she remembered it. It was important to Ernesta that she had been the first in a line of small girls who reversed a perilous situation because she had been the one called on to think up the solution. She wondered if this being first in line would happen to her again, was that the kind of person she was.

All the people of the Snake clan of transformation had great control in physical matters, in this family they had learned it from Ernesta's grandmother, the great Mundane, who was on a lasting journey. She had left behind her five children in the city, four women and a man, Blueberry Jon. Of the four sisters the youngest was Ernesta's mother Donna and the elder three were her formidable aunts.

Ernesta examined the pattern of jars and scratches she had made to help herself recall what had happened on the particular day. There was one element missing, something so mysterious she had discussed it with nobody, not even her mother who sometimes listened or appeared to be doing so, under her lowered eyelids and nodding skull.

Of all the dreamers in the city Ernesta's mother Donna was the most unusual. While other women dreamed their children from stars, events or people, she had dreamed hers from a strange plant growing deep in some rocky hills east of the city. Someday Ernesta would meet this plant, who was called by her mother a spirit mate and called by her aunts a greedy little weed.

Anyone has a genius, a spirit double who represents the best of oneself. Donna's genius is a weed living tenuously miles from the city on an outcropping of alkaline rocks. Having dreamed her first and only child while looking at it one midnight, naming it her spirit mate she brought parts of its leaves home to show her family. Thereafter her sisters harped so long on its uselessness she stopped her visits to the rocks shortly after Ernesta was born but lately had taken to making them once again. Dreaming of wild vegetables she keeps her charms in leather sacks under her pillow, practicing a nighttime skill of transformation that has to do with herself. She is not a member of any councils or groups and not particularly close to any people, avoiding the slipshod everyday political life of the city which so entices her older sisters.

"Ernesta," she whispers, "sometime we will go meet the spirit mate who caused me to dream of you. Then you will never again be satisfied."

Ernesta can see the top of the moon temple where her mother, the youngest of four Snake clan sisters nods over her poppies; she is a charming woman who devotes most of her power to herbs and certain animals rather than to people. She is also an expert at disappearing, vanishing into sleep during the day or into the moon temple tending sprouts and captured snakes while entrancing herself with dreams.

Having many charms some of which are dangerous, she teaches them to her daughter surreptitiously, sometimes taking Ernesta with her on early morning visits to the river bank which thrives and thrashes with living matter. Here they practiced some of the secrets of disappearing, which are used by many kinds of animals for different purposes. The art of disappearing was the first step in any transformation her mother said, to disappear in one form and only then to reappear in another.

"Watch me," she would say at the start of the lesson, how could anyone watch someone who didn't intend to be there any more, but "watch me," her mother would say and then she would disappear as easily as a guinea hen.

"Everything takes up its own space," the charming woman said, "but then there are spaces in between things which are not often used. If you slip into one of those, nothing can notice you." It was a way of becoming neutral. It is very important to know ways of becoming neutral if you often handle poisonous snakes and in this she was an expert. They were a part of her charms.

The aunts do not approve of any of these habits; they say Ernesta will simply become a charming woman and have no social life if she follows the ways of her mother.

A full Snake clan person, they say, has bearing and balance. A full Snake clan person of transformation and balance sings well with understanding of harmony, and knows the physics of all the people and creatures together as well as separately, to say nothing of minerals, water and crystals.

Ernesta is talking to herself softly so as not to disturb Aunt One's basket song. Not drawing the attention of three acute aunts is a hazardous skill though necessary. Someday she would become an expert at disappearing. They have lately been negative in their remarks; they have noticed Ernesta's whimsical tendencies and are bound to correct them. They often use the word, 'responsibility' and use it to balance with 'whimsy.'

"I would rather be like my mother," Ernesta thinks. "She always dances and bushes understand her. My mother laughs as often as a duck."

"Your mother is whimsical," say the aunts, and their mouths droop when they say this. "A full Snake clan person does not use her life for whimsy."

The three aunts are gossips by profession, transferring news, opinions and advice along with poultices, diets, splints, teeth, teas and other condiments for comfortable harmonic living. Their brother Blueberry Jon is a pharmaceutical grinder and mixer of their household.

He is a man of transformation among the shepherds and other men of the out lands, and they sometimes come to ask favors of him. He gives his favors to them and they in turn give him presents. When he stays in the city he does not spend his nights with his sisters and their children very often, going instead to the house of a woman named Gedda of the Barley clan, or over to the men's lodge to spend time talking to the fellows of the Arrow Society.

Ernesta has scraped a deep swathing band in her drawing pattern on the ground, a sweeping cut flowing past the jars with their names, and this is the river. Tracing the side of her hand down the line of it, she stops at the bending part, thinking about the element which is missing from her picture; how can she tell about it? Cautiously she draws a circle with two dots, then stops. Who is there to tell about what she and Margedda saw that day when it bothers her so much and she has no words for it.

Her mother would listen, and say nothing; her mother so rarely spoke, and when she did she so often bent to Ernesta's ear whispering.

"Something about the child is different from what you might think," she would drop this idea into the household quietly, wrapped by its insidious softness around the clattering opinions of the aunts, sly as silk the idea would crawl across the floor and wrap around and around the conversation until the aunts thought they had thought it.

"Ernesta has an odd way of solving problems," she would say one day, and the aunts would stare briefly at the ordinary rectangular shaped child with her wandering eye before continuing with their constant comments on other clan affairs. But by evening they would have tested her with a dozen problems, searching for what was different in her solutions.

"Phoo," Aunt Two would say, "I don't see anything different."

"Don't be so sure," Aunt Three answered, "you know what they say. A woman with a wandering eye can cause a dry spell."

Ernesta's mother is not sleeping today, she is working up in the cool greenhouse in the second story of the Moon temple. She feels deeply related to the plants, she says they are more individual to her than animals or humans; she says sometimes they speak to her of their confinement. The three aunts believe it is contrary to the nature of the world to carry a sensitive nature to such extremes. They also believe that it is the nature of plants to love confinement; rootless mobility, they say, is what a plant hates most. Why else do trees shriek in the wind if not in terror of losing their roots?

Ernesta licked the little bubbles of salty water that formed on her upper lip and underneath her big lower lip. She did not know how to disappear without her mother. She did not know how to describe bothersome things to anyone, even in pictures. She did not know how to draw the spirit of an idea to herself. The air hummed with sunshine, a buzzing noise that seemed to come from the ground. Like the air the inside of Ernesta is acutely buzzing, aware of sights and sounds, motions and meanings, even if she cannot draw the pictures of them yet too well.

From her mother she is understanding empathy and variation in all things; from her Aunt's determination, ruthless self-examination, exactness in all things. From her uncle she is learning deliberation, for Blueberry Jon could take four hours to mix three powders together, much to the scorn of the Aunts, who considered such deliberation irrelevant in a transformational person.

"Why does he have to think about it so much?" they asked each other. "Two pinches of the first, three of the second, four of the third; does it take so much thinking to count from two to four?" But Ernesta watched the ponderosity with fascination. She loved slowness in things, and minute quantities given their due in the course of human afternoons and illnesses.

"Too much whimsy," the Aunts say of their youngest sister Donna, and their mouths droop in Ernesta's direction. "Too much deliberation," they say of their brother Jon, and their mouths droop in the direction of their mother Mundane's closed-off room as though she alone is responsible. "Too much whimsy and too much deliberation do not make a full transformational woman."

All three of her Aunts have philosophical opinions which are for everyday use, and which are certain in their minds from a long time ago. Ernesta is certain they would not even bother to answer a question about whether it is possible to be whimsical and useful too.

Ernesta knows that her aunts want her to become a full transformational woman. Her own mouth droops toward herself when she thinks this. She is afraid that means she would become more like them: square shaped and stern, and terrifying to children. The Aunts laugh in prescribed patterns and are seldom wrong. Seen from underneath, their great protruding jaws are cluttered with teeth and guttered below with wrinkles of brown skin running down to their necks, and little black or white hairs grow on the edges of their chins in long simple strands that wiggle up and down as they talk.

Why is it not possible, Ernesta wonders, to be whimsical and useful too. She lowers her head over the row of jars while her wandering eye darkens, shooting off to the left in a frenzy of hard wondering. Even in Aunt One's half-muffled basket song Ernesta seems to hear her name: "Ernesta, do something useful. Are you doing something useful? Are you learning to count, are you thinking about the names of herbs, are you remembering songs?"

Hearing some loud humming, she looks around. Her second Aunt, Aunt Two, stands in the doorway with her hands held out stiffly in front of her. Aunt Two's hands are always dripping something, wet clay or wet corn meal or wet paint. All three Aunts have strong square shaped hands with thick fingers and a muscle that bumped up at the side of their thumbs, from all the handy work they did all the time. Besides the usual pounding and grinding and lifting that anybody did, Aunt One had a muscle from making baskets with tightly coiled and tied material, Aunt Two's muscle made big thick pots and Aunt Three's muscle made expert false teeth held together with flattened strips of metal and tiny nails.

Aunt One has climbed out of her basket to fetch more wickers from the soaking bowl.

The basket has gotten higher; it now consists of three tall sapling willows wound around and bound together with themselves by thousands of strands of wet and dyed wickers. Aunt One's finest weave contains thirty-four stitches to the inch. The saplings are strong and springy, thick as Ernesta's wrist at the butt, then tapering to the thickness of two of her fingers. They always want to straighten out again; they cannot bear their confinement. They are as hard to hold in position as it is to hold a struggling calf. Aunt One must use the whole length of her arm as well as her tight muscled hands to hold them, Aunt Two says Aunt One will get calluses up to her elbows.

Aunt Two's jaw is working.

"What are you doing outside why aren't you napping?"

"Oh," Ernesta said, "I am just waiting for something to happen."

"Nothing will happen," Aunt Two said.

"Oh you never can tell," called Aunt One. "Everything always changes."

"Nothing ever changes," Aunt Two said, shaking her messy hands. "And I'm glad for that. I love the peace of it all." To Aunt Two change meant disorder and disorder meant evil and that took up a lot of time. Aunt Two does not like to give up her time.

"Oh yes it does," Aunt One said, vigorously nodding. She swatted the thick wet wickers against the ground.

"No," Aunt Two said. "Nothing ever does change, everyone knows that."

Aunt One held the wet wicker strands in her mouth as she climbed on her short stool over the wall of her basket. "Yef ik dudds," she said speaking through the wickers.

"No," Aunt Two said, shaking her hands and going back into the house.

"Yef," sang Aunt One from inside her handy work.

"Ernesta" is an excerpt from a novel-in-progress entitled *Mundane's World*.

The Love Chapter

MARTHA WATERS

*W*ed. 24 Sept. 1969
At last I'm in Europe....
Now I've got to figure out what the hell I'm going to do while
I'm here. Thanks to my mother's unswerving belief that God
wants me for a missionary, I'm surrounded by Christians once
again. She's been praying non-stop for years—double time
since I dropped out of school—and I'm sure this place is the
answer she's been waiting for. She went back to Kansas yesterday and now I'm sort of on my own in the Swiss Alps. This
community is a place she heard about from someone who visited our church and all the way over here she kept repeating that
it's a place "people like you go to." I think she meant there are a
lot of hippies who work here or come to study with Dr. Sievers.
It seems to be a fairly well-organized religious camp with a ten-
dency to Praise the Lord after every sentence. But at least
everyone speaks English and so far all the people I've met are
fairly interesting as long as I ignore the Jesus talk. I wonder if
I'll be able to handle three months of it, though.

Thurs. 25 Sept.
They needed volunteers to work in the gardens so that's what
I'll be doing in the mornings. There's nothing I hate more than
working in a garden so why did I volunteer? Mom will see it as

a sure sign from God that I'm seeing the light. When I was a kid she'd say "the Lord has no respect for idle hands, Emily Louise," as she sent me out to weed her flower garden. It ruined my time in my tree house all summer long because all I could see when I sat up there was how high the weeds were growing around mom's chrysanthemums.

I guess I want to be outdoors so I can keep an eye on the mountains — as if they're going to disappear. I can't get used to them always being there and every time I look out across the valley to the peaks on the other side, it's like noticing someone who's been watching me. Hard to explain. They're always in the way of the horizon but how could anybody mind since they're so beautiful it takes your breath away? I can think of little else but just being in the alps.

To get to the gardens you have to walk almost a mile up a path that is used mostly by cows. They sleep in little barns built under the houses in the village then walk up this path in the morning to graze all day. The clanking of their bells is my new alarm clock. And when I hear them coming back home in the evening I know it's time to go help in one of the kitchens for dinner. I think I have never heard such fine music before as the random counterpoint of cowbells ringing out from mountain pastures. Plenty of reason to enjoy the garden. From the looks of things, we'll be eating an awful lot of Swiss chard this month.

In the afternoons I'm supposed to study tapes of Dr. Sievers' lectures in the tape library under the chapel. I sit by a big window that looks out across the valley. What a marvelous distraction. My ears get tired of Dr. S.'s voice after about an hour. It has such a high-pitched, grating edge and the more excited he gets about his subject the more irritating his voice becomes. I'm supposed to have dinner tomorrow night at his châlet because he and Mrs. S. have all new people eat around their table at least once. It's a tradition from the time when the community was small enough to fit around one table. I'm curious to see what a man with a voice like this looks like. I think he might be very small and very brittle.

The list of lectures goes on for days. I picked one called

"Today's Christian and Rock Music," hoping there might be more music than talk. Half way through the lecture about how rock music is a tool of the devil, Bob Dylan's song "Lay, Lady, Lay" was played in its entirety. It's been so long since I've heard any regular music that I sort of went wild and kept rewinding the tape to listen again and again, turning up the volume a little every time. The proctor came over and asked if there was something wrong with my headset. Apparently, the music was being heard by everyone in the room and someone had complained. "Are you sure this is one of *our* tapes?" the proctor whispered in my ear. So much for Bob Dylan. Someone should tell Dr. S. that Dylan writes folk music, not rock music.

I wish I had the nerve to start traveling around on my own. I guess the fact that I only have 50 dollars in my pocket and don't speak any languages has something to do with my hesitance to take off hitchhiking like I think about all the time. From what I've seen of this community so far it seems like a lot of people stop over for just a few days and then disappear on their way to some other country. So within three months there will be hundreds who will not stay on very long and surely I'll find *someone* to hook up with. Someone who's fluent in French, Italian, German and Greek and plans to spend the winter on an island in the Mediterranean. Yes, that would be perfect.

Fri. 26 Sept.

Dinner with Dr. & Mrs. Sievers was a lot like the last supper, everything was so symbolic. Dr. at one end, Mrs. at the other, and eight strangers on the sides. We read the bible and prayed for 15 minutes before eating and while we ate, Dr. S. answered questions about his religious philosophy in a formal lecture way. We all sat and politely listened while we chewed our food. One woman with a burning need to understand something, hung on his every word and stared at him constantly through a thoughtful squint. She didn't eat at all, just picked up a forkful then always had an urgent question midway to her mouth. She nodded vigorous approval of Dr. Sievers' epistemology, trying to interrupt him with "Yes, but don't you agree

that ... Yes, of course, but why is it that...?" I don't know what
her question was. You have to be quick to get a complete sentence in at these tables. I've never heard the term apologetics
used so often. It seems an ironic choice to describe religious
opinion. I'll have to look it up. And oh my god that VOICE of
his is almost worse live than on tape. He *is* a little man who
oddly resembles an Airedale, in a rather fastidious way. I don't
mean to insult him but when he speaks it's either a high-pitched
whine or a clipped bark and his grey goatee bounces up and
down with nervous precision. I'll have to figure out some way
to keep this from driving me crazy. Everything around here
revolves around this man and respect for him is as much a pre-
supposition as the biblical "fact" of the virgin birth.

Mrs. Sievers wasn't feeling well so she left the table after the
first prayer. She seems nice but was having a hard time concen-
trating and just smiled weakly when anything was said to her. I
don't know why she bothered coming down at all except that it
seems to be an unbreakable rule that everyone knows who the
main mother and father of the community are. I guess that
means I'm now an official part of the family because I've sat at
their table. Something tells me I won't see that much of either
of them beyond this meal, however. They're both very busy
and travel around giving speeches or spend all their time
writing books.

Someone asked Dr. S. why he didn't pastor a church. He
went into a long history of the community and how God called
him to minister to the troubled, drugged-out, alcoholic youth of
the world by opening up his own living room to them. "I've had
my drapes set on fire and my carpet covered with vomit but I
still believe this is what the Lord wants me to do." Everything is
always so dramatic and intense around here. I sort of lost my
appetite.

There was a young woman who kept shooting me glances
across the table, usually at the same time something half-way
funny was said. I mean funny in a self-righteous way, I guess,
because no one dares laugh out loud unless everyone else is
laughing too. I wanted to talk to her after dinner but she

jumped up before dessert, whispered something to Dr. S. and ran out of the room. Dr. S. motioned to my roommate Cynthia, who was milling about in the kitchen, and she followed this person out the door. Everyone seems to have a private mystery here and it reminds me a bit of the atmosphere of a mental hospital. Only it's like a spiritual ward where every waking moment is spent working on or, for some, fighting the state of one's soul. Dr. Sievers is the head psychiatrist who knows the way we should think in order to get into heaven — or out of hell, depending on the way you look at it. And he's smart enough to prove it all through the bible in an intellectual way. Just having to call him Dr. Sievers all the time puts him in a white coat to me.

Saturday 27 September 1969

I wasn't going to tell anyone it's my birthday except that I ran into the woman I wanted to talk with after dinner last night. She pulled it out of me just by singing a song. I was on my way back from a walk and she was sitting by the road playing a guitar. Like an elf on a toadstool. She was singing the Judy Collins song "What I'll Give You Since You Asked" and didn't stop when she saw me. I sat down to listen and she started glowing — maybe it was the angle of the sun but I swear a yellow light framed her body. She sang and studied me as if I were a tree. I watched her left hand slide up and down the guitar's neck, the strings squeaking between each stroke. When she finished the song she still didn't say anything so I started watching the mountains. Down below us I noticed a white glider soaring silently on warm currents rising from the valley. When I pointed it out to her she broke the silence with a cry of delight and hopped up and down the road exclaiming "This is the neatest thing I've ever seen in my life! Wow! Look at it!" etc. etc. for quite a few minutes. Then I said "Hello my name is Emily but people call me Em" and she shook me by the shoulders and laughed a loud raucous laugh that echoed back from the mountains. "*You* can call me Nova."

From there we went to the village pub to celebrate my birthday. Thank goodness it was Sat. afternoon or I would have been hooked up to a tape recorder and that VOICE. Nova doesn't have to work or study, I guess. At least she doesn't have a regular schedule like most of us. I asked her why she's here and she told me this long story about calling off her wedding at the last minute and having a nervous breakdown because she couldn't cope with all the plans. Her parents are friends of Dr. S. so this is where they sent her to recover. The way she told the story was very funny to me and I couldn't stop laughing. Neither could she, after a while.

I'm sure the pub is off limits to us of the community since it's not being a good Christian to drink anything. Alcohol, I mean. But those few beers we drank today were a communion all their own. And it was the best birthday I've ever had. And I've found a new friend, I think. Nova had to go to an appointment that she was almost late for. It was to talk to one of the main counselors — the one she sees on weekends. Apparently she sees Dr. or Mrs. Sievers during the week in what she referred to as "marathon brainwashing." I assumed she was joking but she got suddenly quiet after mentioning it. Then she disappeared up the hill.

At 8:08 pm I turned 22. How does one turn such a thing?

Sun. 28 Sept.

Everybody gets into a festive spirit on Sunday mornings. Church starts at 11 but people gather outside the chapel as early as 10. The weather is as perfect as anyone could dream — bright blue skies, temperatures in the mid 70s, air so clear it crackles. In the mountains above us there's beginning to be a change in color and it's starting to drip its way down toward the valley, which is still green. Reds, yellows, oranges and browns mixed like a Monet canvas. It will be a daily litany of change from top to bottom now until Halloween.

There was such a crowd coming to the service that it was considered gracious of me to offer to stand on the balcony that circles three sides of the sanctuary. I leaned against a corner railing and studied the mountains and watched birds fly above and below me.

The obvious magic of this community reaches an almost solid form when they all come together in one room and sing at the top of their lungs. A joyful noise indeed. There's a little organ in the chapel — one keyboard and several rows of pipes that come right out of the top of the case. It can raise quite a racket when all the stops are pulled. On Fri. I timed my study break so I could come up here on the balcony while someone practiced. It gave the perfect Baroque touch to this incomparable view. What in the world could be more exquisite? I can't imagine.

Anyway, so many people gathered together with a common spirit is an electrifying experience to behold and I can understand why this feeling of pure elation is what Christians love more than anything else. It's what they live for. When the singing starts it would not surprise me to see the roof levitate itself above the mountains. After about 10 minutes of singing, Dr. Sievers steps up to the pulpit to put a cap on all that energy with one of his sermons. And he rises to the occasion with resounding fury by pacing across the stage like Mick Jagger, pounding his bible and warning us all that God is not especially pleased with the world. He clamps a heavy grip of morality onto each individual soul and at the end bids everyone to go out into the world and preach the gospel. Then we sing again and break loose from all containment. It is the music that's the most holy force of all, I believe.

Afterward I had a short chat with Cynthia, whose feet were not touching the ground. We sort of floated around each other with C. saying things like "I think my heart is bursting with love — aren't we lucky to be so close to Christ Himself?" I asked her if she'd seen Nova today and she said "Who?" When I described Nova she said "Oh you mean Susan — I think she's sick again and staying in bed." With that she floated off to talk with other friends.

I went to pay Nova a visit but her bed was empty and no one was around. She lives in the farthest châlet at the edge of the village. The back door of her room opens out to a patio full of geraniums in big, long boxes plus an unobstructed view of the valley. Gloria, the head gardener and my work supervisor, is one of her roommates. I haven't met the others yet.

In all there are seven châlets that are part of Dr. S.'s community and they're dispersed throughout the three tiers of this little French-speaking village. What must the villagers think of the constant stream of English and American kids traveling in packs up and down their streets at all hours of the day or night? Some of us look pretty scroungy, I must admit. I've learned a few words of French so I can at least say hello when I pass the men with their cows. I rarely see any women but I can feel them looking out at me from inside their houses.

Mon. 29 Sept.

The name Susan comes up often—or maybe I'm just noticing it when it's said now. Several people here have that name so it takes a while before I know who's being referred to. I don't blame Nova for using a name other than Susan—she's not a Susan at all to me. And I can't imagine calling her Sue or Susie either. But when I call her Nova nobody knows who I'm talking about at first. That makes it all the more special somehow— like I know a different person than everybody else does.

I asked Gloria if Nova had been sick and she said "Do you mean Susan? Not really." That was about all I could get her to say. We walked up to the gardens together this morning because we had to carry these huge baskets for the vegetables. It was starting to rain a little so we had to hurry.

Tues. 30 Sept.

The most remarkable thing happened during last night's bible study in my room. I still don't quite know what to make of it and Nova woke up this morning totally disoriented, remembering absolutely nothing that had happened. For a minute she couldn't even figure out who I was—or at least I think that's what I saw in her eyes. She looked like a frightened little animal as she disappeared out the door without a word.

Four of my five roommates are the type of Christians who

175

feel the need to be doing something holy all the time so they discuss scripture every night before bed. Since they're all saved already, they think of it as missionary training and get into lively debates about the best way to introduce the bible to heathens. If they knew the level of my skepticism I fear they might turn all that energy toward me so I try to keep my real opinions to myself or come home late enough to miss the meeting entirely.

Last night, however, I was on my top bunk writing postcards and studying the map of the Mediterranean that covers the wall next to my pillow. Cynthia is reading one of Paul's letters to the Corinthians this week and it was I Cor:13 we were focusing on, also known as the Love Chapter. Cynthia feels this is a perfect place to begin explaining the love of Jesus to a non-believer. I've always liked that chapter so I was half interested in hearing how this group interpreted it. Just as C. finished reading the seventh verse — "Love bears all things, believes all things, hopes all things, endures all things." — there was a soft knock at the door. It was Nova looking for me and C. invited her to join the group. Everyone is a potential convert to C., especially someone with a troubled past. I motioned for Nova to climb up and sit with me on my bunk, trying not to seem alarmed by her appearance. She looked terrible — her hair all tangled up, her face white as the moon and her jacket buttoned up wrong. Her hands shifted constantly from pocket to pocket and her eyes darted all over the room without seeing anything. She crumpled up beside me and I nodded to C. that things were probably okay so please just continue with the meeting. Bless her for going on without a fuss. As the bible study picked up again I concentrated on Nova's condition and tried to get her calmed down somehow.

I think if Nova could have crawled inside of me she would have. She kept huddling in closer and closer and I just opened up my arms until she found the way she wanted to hold on to me. Then I wrapped my arms around her and held on tight. She was in a weird trance I didn't understand but it was obvious she needed a lot of comfort and that's easy to give. What a mess of nerves she was.

While the group continued on with the Love Chapter I stroked Nova's back and tried to untangle her hair. Every muscle in her body was tensely locked. Jennifer, our newest roommate, was struggling with "When I was a child, I spoke like a child, I thought like a child, I reasoned like a child." She said she never had time to be a child when she was a child because she was the oldest of seven kids and their mother died so she doesn't know what it _means_ to be a child. It's hard for me to imagine that since I'm the baby of our family and never had to take care of anyone younger than myself. Everything gets so infinitely complicated when dealing with simple truth. I looked at Nova and wondered what she was like when she was a kid. She probably turned sixteen at the age of six.

By the time the meeting ended Nova had relaxed into a deep sleep. Cynthia checked in on us and stood with her hand on Nova's shoulder for a minute, studying her like a puzzle. I whispered that we should let her rest and C. nodded agreement, whispering back "She wrestles with many demons. If you need any help just let me know."

Then the lights went out and I just held Nova in my arms for the rest of the night. She hardly stirred at all and my body grew painfully stiff but I didn't dare move for fear I might disturb her sleep. It reminded me of a time when I was eleven or twelve. Mom and my sister and I were on vacation in the Ozarks and we went driving way up into the hills to visit a distant relative I'd never heard of — someone's great aunt. She had a beautiful house made of glass and stone and there was a huge tree growing up in the middle of the living room. She had adopted an old tomcat called Foster that had one ear missing and a coat like a worn out S.O.S. pad. He didn't like anybody. My sister tried to pet him and he bit her. But he walked up to me, sat down in my lap and started purring. I was so honored and everyone else was so shocked that I let him sleep for hours like he wanted to — all curled up so I could scratch him behind his good ear and smooth out his ratty tail. I was sitting cross-legged on the floor and thought I would die if I couldn't move my feet out from under me. But I didn't disturb old Foster until we had to leave.

Nova is indeed struggling with some very dark forces. Whether or not they are demons like Cynthia says remains to be seen, I suppose. Christians see the devil in almost everything sometimes. Maybe I can help her somehow. I hope so. She seems to like me a lot and I guess that's a good beginning. I hope I know what I'm doing.

"The Love Chapter" is an excerpt from a novel-in-progress presently titled *Journal of a Plebian Witch.*

The Tree on
The Mountain

DEENA METZGER

Dinah, daughter of Jacob by Leah, was ravished by
Shechem, a Hivite. For that reason, and with the help of a
peculiarly low cunning, Simeon and Levi, Dinah's own
brothers, revenged the insult. What Dinah thought of the
whole matter is not recorded.
                        —Old Testament glossary, King James Version

*M*y name is Dinah. It is a desert name. My father was
Jacob and I was his only daughter, the only soft flesh, the only
breasts to bud from his leathery hands. Who would have
thought that he could have a daughter, but it was in his old age
when his limbs were also beginning to soften as if they had been
chewed, as hide is, by the teeth of time. Because I am a
woman, I was not taught to kill. To everything that happened,
until now, I have only been a witness.

And Dinah, the daughter of Leah, which she bore unto
Jacob, went out to see the daughters of the land, to dance
and to beat drums. And when Shechem, the Hivite Prince,
the son of Hamor, saw her, he was overcome with love and
he lay with her.

Do you know about names? Do you think a name is sound? A name is alive, has a life far longer than a life. It persists in its own form, drags itself through the centuries, cannot be killed, rarely dies out. My name is an alert night creature, has the tenacity of vines wedged into the crevices of unyielding stone, the parading stubbornness of ants, the radiant expansion of bees; it persists. My name is not just a name, is not merely a call. It is the poison kernel which sprouts again and again wherever it falls. A hemlock, Deena, will not birth a goat. And you who come out of Dinah are Dinah again. Dinah is irrevocably Dinah to the end of time. Our name means 'well,' means 'water out of the earth, scarce but sweet,' or Dinah means 'bitterness,' or it means 'judged.'

> Shechem saw her and he took her and lay with her and he defiled her.

Dinah is the desert, is harsh, inhospitable, substantial and enduring. Sometimes Dinah is tents and skins, sometimes she is the mercilessly shaped rock. Once I did not exist, but afterwards Dinah exists for all time. I reproduce myself like any other endangered but surviving species. In those who are born of me, I persist.

I am Dinah. I loved a Heathen. My brothers killed him. It was thousands of years ago.

> And Shechem's soul cleaved unto Dinah, the daughter of Jacob, and he loved the damsel. And Shechem spoke unto his father, Hamor, saying, "Get me this damsel to wife."

Dinah is the desert, the merciless sun, the grit.

> And the sons of Jacob answered Shechem and Hamor deceitfully, and said, "We cannot do this thing, to give our sister to one that is uncircumcised; for that were a reproach unto us. But in this will we consent unto you: if you will be as we be, that every male of you be circumcised; then will we give our daughters unto you and we will take your daughters to us and we will dwell with you and we will become one people.

Dinah is the turned wine, the spoiled meat, the parched skin. Dinah is the mirage and the dry well.

And every Hivite male was circumcised and it came to pass on the third day when they were sore that two of the sons of Jacob, the brothers of Dinah by Leah, took each man his sword and came upon the city boldly and slew all the males. And they slew Hamor and Shechem, his son, with the edges of their swords. And they took Dinah out of Shechem's house. And they spoiled the city and even all that was in the house and took their wealth and their little ones and their wives.

I know what is happening and what is coming. This has happened before.

•

Dear Shechem:

So far I have failed you. In the actual living out of events, I have not yet been equal to the task. And so I am beginning again, in the only way I know, to conjure a world. This story is for you. It is of the first order of magic: from my desire, I will conjure you; from my love, I will conjure you; in this writing, I will conjure you.

The writer is always between the beginning and the end of the world and she must write in both directions at once, back and forth, so that the past and future coincide in one seed. And so I create and cancel time so we may meet in that desert where I hear the spirits can live.

When I first went to Nablus—they have taken your name from the city and given it this modern name—you were not there and so this story is, first of all, for you. You were the one I had gone to meet. But even as I was disembarking from the airplane in Israel and later driving with the other two upon the dusty road to Nablus, I thought it was hopeless. After all that effort, I was afraid even in my heart that it was madness and that the end of the journey would be only such much stone and ruins as I had already imagined.

I have been trying to tell this story for months and each turn

I have undermined myself by not recognizing the task. I wanted to tell you what happened though I assume events of the material world are of no interest to spirits and gods. But as I come to see the challenge, it seems as if I also have permission to proceed. What happened, what didn't happen, what could have happened, what needed to happen, what will happen, what must happen, must blend into the moment when I walk away from my friend Raquel and from Eli the guide, through the archway in the ancient wall toward the altar in the center of Shechem and stand there disbelieving, trying to make sense of the dishonored site, the broken stones. I stand there staring, faithless, without suspecting the moment will be redeemed, as you come across the dry and empty earth, past the shards and fragments, the bits of temple and floor, and recognize me as certainly as if we have met before. As you walk toward me, your dark brown eyes stare into mine, equally dark. Scrutinizing me, you are either rude or familiar, you say, "Don't you remember?"

No, Shechem, the task is more difficult, is beyond me, not only in the realization, but also in the conception. Still, she, who is directing this act, is not constrained by the limits of my understanding. Sometimes, like God, in the act of creation, we try to create a world. Of course, like God, we fail. Still, like God, we attempt it blindly, for it is in the moment of conception that it comes to be. Before conception? Nothing. There is no blueprint, research, experiment, no painstakingly slow procedure of trial and error. Before—there is nothing and afterwards—everything.

Something, Shechem, is to be rewritten, something is to be retold, something is to be relived. Somewhere at the end of this journey, something and someone will be altered. I thought it would be a simple task—I would recreate our history but also avoid its consequences. I thought I might achieve this through evasion. As once I submitted a film script to my producers with three different conclusions, I simply wanted to bring our story to another conclusion. I simply want to tell it so that at the end, Shechem, you won't die and I won't remain alone, so that at the end of this retelling, you won't die again.

But now, I am beginning to realize how very carefully, I must tell this, how I must set down each word as an invocation, so that at the end, the very story which created us, which I have come to live again, will, indeed, be erased, transformed. Then my name will no longer carry this pain. I do not want to live out my name again and again. I want to be certain that all the Deenas who come after me will not continue to suffer Dinah's fate.

•

When we were half way up Mount Sinai, I stopped. I pretended it was fatigue, insisting that Raquel go on ahead because she was afraid she'd miss the dawn and I was afraid I was moving so quickly that I would miss everything. I was only anxious that the others on the tour would catch up to me and that I'd be swallowed up in their chatter. Gadi had taken us ahead in a small jeep he was going to use to bring supplies to the monastery, so we had a jump on everyone else, but not enough for me to be safe. Far below I could see their flashlights flickering like lightning bugs but the wind drowned out the sound of their voices. I couldn't create enough silence or enough time. I envied Moses all the time he had, despite Gadi's derision. And Dinah, she had all the time she needed, too much time crossing the desert behind Joseph, but time enough to clear the death out of her so that she could arrive in Egypt clean. In less than twenty-four hours, I was already drying like a gourd, rubbed white powder from my skin, the first sign of being reduced. I put everything I came across into my mouth for the dry taste, the metal, the hermetically clean sand, the old, old salt. The Israelites needed forty years, two generations to clear out memory. One generation in order to forget everything and then another generation in order to remember what was under the forgetting. Forty years in order to forget what we had remembered in order to forget. Forty years in order to remember what was originally forgotten.

Like I forgot you, Shechem, for my entire life, I forgot you.

183

And for how many lifetimes before that?

And Dinah, all that time remembering. What a task. Remembering against all odds and all oppressions, inhibitions and prohibitions. With even a little remembering we are crazed, only a little remembering makes us mad, a little more remembering and it begins to show, as with pregnancy you can only wear girdles so long and soon the world says, "there goes a crazy lady, look she's talking to herself," [there's no one else to talk to], Dinah remembered for lifetimes. Raquel calls me obsessed. Dinah, Dinah, there is obsession. That's devotion. I'm not as dedicated as you are, Dinah. I'm an American woman, we know a lot about physical training, aerobics, that kind of extremis, but when it comes to spiritual discipline, we take a break and go to the movies.

I didn't have forty years or even forty minutes before the tourists and guides would catch up to us. I didn't want to walk with anyone, not even with Svika who could have pointed out everything of interest because he knew this mountain the way Gadi knew the desert. He was agile, had climbed each of its faces in each season. While I was standing there trying to ignore the little sparks of light which were coming closer — in the Kaballah it says that in order to free the world of evil, we must free the sparks of the shattered god imprisoned in dense matter. Every act of Tikkun redeems the world. —

> Evil, as Luria saw it, was the result of ancient events in Azilut, the highest World, where the seven lowest Sefirot, unable to contain the flow of Divinity, shattered, causing the Worlds below to sink beneath their true level.
> —Kabbalah, Z'ev ben Shimon Halevi, p. 72

— I thought that if God had appeared, I would have been irritated so desirious was I to be alone. The little lights distracted me so I sat down against a twisted dry tree so that I could see the others when they approached but was staring not down the mountain but across the path onto what I presumed was its stone face. It was so dark, I could barely see the two or three feet across, only the rough floor of the path, some pebbles about my feet, the slight sheen of my white shoes, the patina of my own skin so that I understood for the first time that on some occasions the human being carries her own light and so we can see in the dark.

For minutes at a time, I managed silence. I erased all history from my thoughts. Shechem you were in another country, Joseph was in Egypt and Dinah had never climbed this mountain, had never asked for scripture. So I had no story to learn or destroy in order to understand. And there was no voice, either large or small, speaking to me, and there was as yet no emptiness.

Not knowing what to do, I got up again and looked at the poor wizened tree with its tenacious leaves and I put my hands up in imitation. I suppose that someone watching me from a distance might have decided I was dancing, because I tried to bend my arms and then my entire body to capture the shape of the tree, curving first along one branch then along another, making thorns and twigs of my fingers, sliding my spine along the very trunk, no more than a human spine itself, and reaching down as the tree reached down so that I pretended that I was as amenable to wind as the tree was.

"There is only one tree on this mountain," Svika was saying. "It's just ahead. A thorn tree. It's the burning bush, some say, where Moses first encountered God. You can't look on the face of God, you know ..." Svika's voice had swollen with his knowledge and was booming across the path though he had still not come around the bend. "... so God showed himself as an unconsuming fire that was held in those very branches. The tree's so dry it should have gone up like tinder. We'll rest here for fifteen minutes and then we'll have to scurry up to the summit like goats to get there before dawn. This isn't a bathroom stop, not even for the men, you'll have to control yourself until we are on the other side."

I was already on the path, scurrying, as Svika suggested. Raquel was far ahead. But even as I rushed forward, I saw that my stride became smaller and speed was more difficult. I was walking as one does in a nightmare when suddenly it is impossible to move as if the air were mud and everything was named resistance. Something held me back, caught in my throat. I was unprotected; we had left no one below to tend the fire and to dance with the golden calf.

It took me two hours to climb the stone snake in the moonless dark up to the chill peaks of Mt. Sinai. I slipped several times, the pebbles sliding out from under my feet, so that finally I had to put the flashlight in my pocket and trust to my eyes to see in the dark.

My eyes accommodated quickly to the night between moons and as we reached the top a bitter wind arose carrying dawn in its mouth, so that when I reached the very peak, the sun rose also and broke open upon the sharp granite, running red and orange across the sky. Someone sang out, "Hal-le-lu-*jah!*" and then we were still. It was the harshest landscape I had ever seen. Harsh as law.

The wind scraped the wounded belly of the sky across the jagged peaks so that it bled again and again, the stain absorbed into the clouds as onto linen and then falling down from the summit, a red rain. Then there was a great fire in the sky, an explosion of every form of light, until the dark was trammeled, the blood expunged, and all that remained of the sky was brilliant white and unbearable blue. I hadn't brought glasses, deliberately, as if I'd known I would have the opportunity to be blinded and I was afraid I'd protect myself from it and so I had to cover my eyes with my hands until I adjusted to the intensity. People deprived of sunlight go mad. Children kept in buildings with only fluorescent light develop learning problems, run around like wild beasts, can't add or subtract. Still, the light can be dangerous.

Behind me someone was humming a little tune and someone else was piping into a small flute. I couldn't turn to see who it was because the wind was so fierce, I had to hold on carefully not to lose my balance and tumble down to the ledges far below. It was very cold, Raquel and I shivered in each other's arms, but we gave each other no warmth. Down below the wind rearranged the sand but here everything was the way it had always been. On this spot, 10,000 feet above the ochre sand floor, Moses had received the law.

The Bavarian ladies arrived, huffing and puffing, formed a little cluster behind Raquel and myself and sang a few hymns in German in Christ's name. I started to silence them, was about to say, "Have respect, you're in Israel, you know," but then I realized we were in Egypt and I didn't believe in one God anyway, so I sat on my displeasure as on an anthill and tried to be grateful for the windbreak they provided and, as I expected, they soon got bored and cold and left Raquel and me alone at the top, shivering in our thin djellabas, with the double snakes, the snake of Crete and silver serpent I'd bought at the Rockefeller museum, a replica of the snake goddess that had been excavated at Shechem, twisting icily against my chest.

Soon Raquel had had enough and I walked with her to the beginning of the stairs cut into the rock which would take us directly down to the monastery but as she started down, I pulled my hand away. "I'll be there soon. Gadi said we'd have a few hours in the monastery itself, so I'll be down before we take off." Raquel moved so as to stay with me, but I motioned her away and she left me and I went up to the top again and looked away from Israel where Dinah had been born to look even deeper into Egypt where Dinah had still to go to die.

Like rusted twisted knives, like the spikes of the maguey, like a trunk split by an axe, like a spear mangled in the heart, like teeth filed to a point, like a tusk thrust through the breast, like splintered bone jutting out of the skin, like thorns growing through the flesh, like bamboo rammed under the fingernail, like a hook in the eye of a fish, like the shriek of metal against stone, the dreadful peaks of this desolate range.

I was pulled down to my knees. It was for this that Shechem had been killed, in this name.

Thou shalt have no other gods before me.

I fingered the snakes the way one fingers worry beads or the rosary, wanting comfort from real things, or the way the aborigines in times of duress are allowed into the sacred hut to finger the churinga to gain power. I knew the snakes were silver, the proportions of metals carefully determined so they would shine sufficiently but not bend too much. I knew they were made by women and were not gods in themselves, everyone had known that from the beginning of time. But where do the gods live? And what does it mean to be a vessel for the gods? And when one shapes a vessel with one's own hands then...? Was an idol or a replica, something like a bit of the holy cross, or the grail, which because of its proximity to the heart sometimes came alive or was it like a temple where on occasion the gods sat? And hadn't it seemed to me so very briefly that I paid no attention to it, that one of the little asherahs remaining in the case glowed for a moment when I looked at it and then the light went out. Of it? Out of my eyes? Will carbon dating find the light in it?

> Thou shalt not make unto thee any graven image, or any likeness of anything that is in heaven above, or that is in the earth beneath, or that is in the water under the earth: thou shalt not bow down thyself to them, nor serve them: for I the Lord thy God am a jealous God, visiting the iniquity of the fathers upon the children unto the third and fourth generation of them that hate me; and showing mercy unto thousands of them that love me, and keep my commandments.

The wind was so savage I could have been blown off the mountain if I didn't wedge myself between two outcroppings, oblivious now to the skin scraped off my hands and knees and face by this face of God.

And when I was ready, I cried. I cried first for Shechem and then for the teraphim and for Rachel and Leah who had both turned from me so that I had no father and no mothers. And I cried for Dinah who had known this through the centuries. And then I put my face down on the stone so that I would mark my forehead on the granite and remember everything and then I heard a voice, speaking, it surprised me, it was my own voice, I was speaking aloud, "I forgive you," it said.

So I got up and ran, not down the stairs yet, not to the cloister of Saint Katherine, but down the steep path, without stopping, until I came to the tree which I could see quite clearly now, it was hard to believe it was alive it had so few leaves, it was twisted and dry and covered with spikes.

But it was a tree. And so it was god. Always had been god, burning or not it was god. I knew her name. I threw up my arms, there was no one around but me and Her and I held them above my head in imitation of her branches, knowing then that this was the way that Dinah had prayed and you, Shechem, had prayed and Joseph had prayed, not kneeling, not scraping our faces in the ground, but standing, in imitation of the god, hands raised in joy, dancing. ASHERAH! And it seemed important to me which god I chose to worship, because the gods are imprinted upon their followers and the jealous gods sow jealousy and the vengeful gods sow vengeance and warlike gods make war. I thought to myself, dancing, this God in the tree, She does no harm.

When I was tired I slipped down and put my back to the tree though a moment before it had been burning as it had burned when Moses had seen Her as it always burned when She revealed herself and had hidden her name in the rock where he had hidden himself from her so that he felt only Her breath, the wind in the tree, as She went by.

"I'm afraid I'll forget," I was anguished. And I could find no words for what I saw. The words bent away from meaning even as the lowest branch bent away from the trunk though the air was still burning with Her though nothing was different from the way it had been.

> The words bent away, they could not say it, could not say what it was she felt, was feeling, was learning that thinking was feeling, that she had been cut off from the thinking, from the feeling of it, that it was manifest, in other worlds, it was alive, thinking was also like an animal or something crawling within her with dimension and temperature, had edges, thinking was like love, or joy, feeling was manifest, in other worlds, it was alive, thinking was also like an animal or something crawling within her with dimension and temperature, had edges, thinking was like love, or joy, feeling was

manifest, and she could not remember this, could only live in the moment, feel it alive in her and then it fell out of her and left not even a shadow or a footstep when she was taken up or down at once into the six dimensions, one by one, until she was simultaneously traveling in all the possible directions at once away from herself, this is not about belief, she thought, this is not about thought, this is not about emotions, it is about knowing, the sexuality, the physicality, the presence of knowing, mind as cock or cunt, the great slit between the worlds where knowing penetrated, she had invented words without language, understanding in six dimensions where mind materialized, was physicalized, was alive with eros, where mind loved, fucked, rollicked, tumbled, cavorted, all this knowledge without words, remembering does not need clothes, the voice said, and the landscape quivered with life, was full of the gods, was the gods. How will I remember this, she wailed desperately, I will remember it, I understand this now because I can feel it. And she could see herself, feel herself, was in that moment also as she would be later trying to remember, and she could feel the frustration of not being able to remember, could feel the forgetting even as she was not forgetting, she was ahead of herself even as she was behind herself even as she was flying also into the other direction where she was no longer herself, she was with Dinah she was knowing everything that Dinah knew, even as she was also a witness and also forgetting, she was knowing it also in the six dimensions and without words for they did not speak the same language, never had, and remembering that she would want to remember, she asked without words, what shall I do, how shall I do it, and Dinah said there were no rules, never had been, there was only the hum and the need to listen to it, to tune oneself so that one was also humming, not making a hum but was the hum itself, the worlds all six of them then made one, conflict makes many which does not see that many is one, make two into one, it is what I did, you will have to have his child, and then you will never forget, even if he dies, even if you fail, you will have the child and he will always be alive, and the two of you together alive, in her child and in her child, passed on, they cannot kill him, of that you can be certain. Have his child.

Then she thought the God came again, it was the sun, it was the tree against her back, she was only a woman only breathing, she understood that, the most difficult one of all. I will understand this, forever, she thought even as it faded from her and she looked up and saw that the sky was innocently blue. The sun was shining. She expected to hear birds.

I climbed to the top and ran across it, didn't even take a last look around, just crossed over and ran down the 3000 stone stairs onto the searing sands of the desert floor. Lizards slithered out of my path from under one rock to another, and a few wild flowers opened white brave faces to the fierce sun.

I knew you were alive, Shechem, somewhere, I had faith, you were alive and I had not conjured you.

"The Tree on The Mountain" is an excerpt from a novel-in-progress entitled *What Dinah Thought.*

She Unnames Them

URSULA K. Le GUIN

*M*ost of them accepted namelessness with the perfect indifference with which they had so long accepted and ignored their names. Whales and dolphins, seals and sea otters consented with particular grace and alacrity, sliding into anonymity as into their element. A faction of yaks, however, protested. They said that "yak" sounded right, and that almost everyone who knew they existed called them that. Unlike the ubiquitous creatures such as rats and fleas, who had been called by hundreds or thousands of different names since Babel, the yaks could truly say, they said, that they had a *name*. They discussed the matter all summer. The councils of the elderly females finally agreed that though the name might be useful to others it was so redundant from the yak point of view that they never spoke it themselves and hence might as well dispense with it. After they presented the argument in this light to their bulls, a full consensus was delayed only by the onset of severe early blizzards. Soon after the beginning of the thaw, their agreement was reached and the designation "yak" was returned to the donor.

Among the domestic animals, few horses had. cared what anybody called them since the failure of Dean Swift's attempt to name them from their own vocabulary. Cattle, sheep, swine, asses, mules, and goats, along with chickens, geese, and turkeys, all agreed enthusiastically to give their names back to the people to whom — as they put it — they belonged.

A couple of problems did come up with pets. The cats, of course, steadfastly denied ever having had any name other than those self-given, unspoken, ineffably personal names which, as the poet named Eliot said, they spend long hours daily contemplating — though none of the contemplators has ever admitted that what they contemplate is their names and some onlookers have wondered if the object of that meditative gaze might not in fact be the Perfect, or Platonic, Mouse. In any case, it is a moot point now. It was with the dogs, and with some parrots, lovebirds, ravens, and mynahs, that the trouble arose. These verbally talented individuals insisted that their names were important to them, and flatly refused to part with them. But as soon as they understood that the issue was precisely one of individual choice, and that anybody who wanted to be called Rover, or Froufrou, or Polly, or even Birdie in the personal sense, was perfectly free to do so, not one of them had the least objection to parting with the lowercase (or, as regards German creatures, uppercase) generic appellations "poodle," "parrot," "dog," or "bird," and all the Linnaean qualifiers that had trailed along behind them for two hundred years like tin cans tied to a tail.

The insects parted with their names in vast clouds and swarms of ephemeral syllables buzzing and stinging and humming and flitting and crawling and tunnelling away.

As for the fish of the sea, their names dispersed from them in silence throughout the oceans like faint, dark blurs of cuttlefish ink, and drifted off on the currents without a trace.

•

None were left now to unname, and yet how close I felt to them when I saw one of them swim or fly or trot or crawl across my way or over my skin, or stalk me in the night, or go along beside me for a while in the day. They seemed far closer than when their names had stood between myself and them like a clear barrier: so close that my fear of them and their fear of me became one same fear. And the attraction that many of us felt, the desire to smell one another's smells, feel or rub or caress one another's scales or skin or feathers or fur, taste one another's blood or flesh, keep one another warm—that attraction was now all one with the fear, and the hunter could not be told from the hunted, nor the eater from the food.

This was more or less the effect I had been after. It was somewhat more powerful than I had anticipated, but I could not now, in all conscience, make an exception for myself. I resolutely put anxiety away, went to Adam, and said, "You and your father lent me this—gave it to me, actually. It's been really useful, but it doesn't exactly seem to fit very well lately. But thanks very much! It's really been very useful."

It is hard to give back a gift without sounding peevish or ungrateful, and I did not want to leave him with that impression of me. He was not paying much attention, as it happened, and said only, "Put it down over there, O.K.?" and went on with what he was doing.

One of my reasons for doing what I did was that talk was getting us nowhere, but all the same I felt a little let down. I had been prepared to defend my decision. And I thought that perhaps when he did notice he might be upset and want to talk. I put some things away and fiddled around a little, but he continued to do what he was doing and to take no notice of anything else. At last I said, "Well, goodbye, dear. I hope the garden key turns up."

He was fitting parts together, and said, without looking around, "O.K., fine, dear. When's dinner?"

"I'm not sure," I said. "I'm going now. With the—" I hesitated, and finally said, "With them, you know," and went on out. In fact, I had only just then realized how hard it would have been to explain myself. I could not chatter away as I used to do, taking it all for granted. My words now must be as slow, as new, as single, as tentative as the steps I took going down the path away from the house, between the dark-branched, tall dancers motionless against the winter shining.

OTHER BOOKS BY THE CONTRIBUTORS:

Becky Birtha: *For Nights Like This One: Stories of Loving Women.* Frog In The Well, East Palo Alto, California, 1983.

Sandy Boucher: *Heartwomen: An Urban Feminist's Odyssey Home.* Harper & Row, New York, 1982.
The Notebooks of Leni Clare and Other Short Stories. Crossing Press, Trumansburg, New York, 1982.

Anne Cameron: *Daughters of Copper Woman.* Press Gang Publishers, British Columbia, 1981.
Earth Witch. Harbour, British Columbia, 1985.
How Raven Freed The Moon. Harbour, British Columbia, 1985.
How The Loon Lost Her Voice. Harbour, British Columbia, 1985.
The Journey. Spinsters/Aunt Lute Books, San Francisco, 1986.

Judy Grahn: *Another Mother Tongue: Gay Words, Gay Worlds.* Beacon Press, Boston, 1984.
The Highest Apple: Sappho and the Lesbian Poetic Tradition. Spinsters, Ink, San Francisco, 1985.
The Queen of Wands. The Crossing Press, Trumansburg, New York, 1982.
The Work of a Common Woman: Collected Poetry (1964-1977). The Crossing Press, Trumansburg, New York, 1984.

Ursula K. Le Guin: *Always Coming Home.* Harper & Row, New York, 1985
The Dispossessed. Avon, New York, 1975.
The Left Hand of Darkness. Harper & Row, New York, 1980.
and many others.

Deena Metzger: *The Axis Mundi Poems.* Jazz Press, Los Angeles, 1981.
A Book of Hags (cassette tape). Watershed Tapes, Washington, D.C., 1976.
Skin: Shadows/Silence. West Coast Poetry Review, Reno, Nevada, 1976.
The Woman Who Slept With Men To Take The War Out of Them and *Tree* (two works in one volume). Wingbow Press, Berkeley, 1983.

continued

OTHER BOOKS BY THE CONTRIBUTORS, continued:

Bode Noonan: *Red Beans and Rice: Recipes for Lesbian Health and Wisdom.* The Crossing Press, Trumansburg, New York 1986.

Judith Stein: A number of short works, both fiction and non-fiction, can be ordered through Bobbeh Meisehs Press, 137 Tremont Street, Cambridge, Ma. 02139. Write for a complete listing.

Merlin Stone: *Ancient Mirrors of Womanhood: A Treasury of Goddess and Heroine Lore From Around the World.* Beacon Press, Boston, 1984.
When God Was A Woman. Harcourt Brace Jovanovitch, San Diego, 1978.

Kitty Tsui: *The Words of a Woman Who Breathes Fire.* Spinsters, Ink, San Francisco, 1983.

The Crossing Press Feminist Series includes the following titles:

Abeng, A Novel by Michelle Cliff

Clenched Fists, Burning Crosses, A Novel by Chris South

Crystal Visions, Nine Meditations for Personal and Planetary Peace by Diane Mariechild

A Faith of One's Own: Explorations by Catholic Lesbians, edited by Barbara Zanotti

Feminist Spirituality and the Feminine Divine, An Annotated Bibliography by Anne Carson

Folly, A Novel by Maureen Brady

Hear The Silence: Stories by Women of Myth, Magic and Renewal, edited by Irene Zahava

Learning Our Way: Essays in Feminist Education, edited by Charlotte Bunch and Sandra Pollack

Lesbian Etiquette, Humorous Essays by Gail Sausser

Lesbian Images, Literary Commentary by Jane Rule

Magic Mommas, Trembling Sisters, Puritans & Perverts, Feminist Essays by Joanna Russ

Mother, Sister, Daughter, Lover, Stories by Jan Clausen

Mother Wit: A Feminist Guide to Psychic Development by Diane Mariechild

Movement, A Novel by Valerie Miner

Natural Birth, Poetry by Toi Derricotte

Nice Jewish Girls: A Lesbian Anthology, edited by Evelyn Torton Beck

The Notebooks of Leni Clare and Other Short Stories by Sandy Boucher

The Politics of Reality: Essays in Feminist Theory by Marilyn Frye

On Strike Against God, A Lesbian Love Story by Joanna Russ

The Queen of Wands, Poetry by Judy Grahn

Red Beans & Rice, Recipes for Lesbian Health and Wisdom by Bode Noonan

Sinking, Stealing, A Novel by Jan Clausen

Sister Outsider, Essays and Speeches by Audre Lorde

Winter's Edge, A Novel by Valerie Miner

Women Brave in the Face of Danger, Photographs of Latin and North American Women by Margaret Randall

The Work of A Common Woman, Poetry by Judy Grahn

Zami: A New Spelling of My Name, Biomythography by Audre Lorde